COMING UP ROSES

COMING UP ROSES

Short stories by women from Wales

Edited by

Caroline Oakley

HONNO MODERN FICTION

Published by Honno
'Ailsa Craig', Heol y Cawl, Dinas Powys
South Glamorgan, Wales, CF6 4AH

A catalogue record for this book is available from The British Library.

ISBN 1 870206 932
EAN 978 1870206 938

The publisher gratefully acknowledges the financial support of the
Welsh Books Council

Cover image: Getty Images
Cover design: G Preston

Printed in Wales by Gomer

Contents

INTRODUCTION

When I came up with the idea for this anthology – and the title – I had in mind a fairly lighthearted and warm collection of stories with a very British bent. What arrived, with the selections more or less suggesting themselves, was a collection that might well also have been titled 'Pushing Up the Daisies'!

I'm delighted with the final shape of *Coming Up Roses*, it really does have something for everyone who has ever enjoyed a garden, felt close to nature or escaped into the greenery. I hope you enjoy reading it, whether in the garden with a glass of rosé, curled up by the fire, seed catalogues at your feet, or sheltering from spring rain. I have loved all my gardens – wild and neglected, colour co-ordinated or full of organic veg – and I love these stories and am sure you will too.

Caroline Oakley
December, 2007

Coming Up Roses

Molly Price

'Come into the garden, Maud.' How can a song, an old one at that, precipitate one into a life-threatening situation? It did me, although the lady in question wasn't Maud but Sadie, luscious, long-limbed and not averse to nookie *al fresco*.

'You've made your bed, lie in it,' my dear wife said, after catching us amid the catmint and chasing off the competition. She spoke as calmly and gently as a maiden aunt, then hammered me with the spade. Lying in it I am, literally. T'wasn't my wish to be dispatched so quickly and before my time, or to be buried in the garden. My wish was to pass away quietly in old age, when all bodily urges are gone, to be cremated and my ashes sprinkled out over the headland to the winds and the ocean and as far away from Jean's regimented garden as possible. Cunning as ever, she set my death scene methodically, carrying the ladder from the shed, smearing some of me onto the bricks and hedging tools and tearfully told the coroner I had been lopping bushes and must have fallen and hit my head on the raised bed wall. I've never lopped a tree in my life, but old Hicks-Moffat believed her. I was shouting, 'Liar, liar!' and waving my arms about, but of course he couldn't hear me.

I had requested that, on my death, my coffin was to be the finest, the best oak available – I wasn't into saving trees and all that rot. My motto was – if you have money, keep as much of it as possible for yourself and flaunt it in other people's faces. I'd earned it for God's sake… But here I am, zipped up in a home-made bloody body bag under the rose bushes. A humanist funeral – I ask you? I wanted the works, vicar, Rock of Ages and the 21st Psalm, and a do at the best hotel in town, but do you know what Jean asked for? 'Wish me luck as you wave me goodbye' and a Branston Pickle sandwich in the kitchen. This is Jean's revenge. Earth to earth – but rather than dust or ashes, I'm compost.

Twenty years we were married, and for nineteen years and eleven months I regretted it. When I fancied seeing a show in London we went to the Chelsea Flower Show. A drive into the country was a visit to a National Trust garden. There's a limit to a man's patience – you can only admire so much topiary shaped like peacocks. On a tour to France, we ended up at Monet's masterpiece. I was bitten to the bone by mosquitoes and I failed to see any beauty in a few flower heads floating in a green scum.

We went our separate ways after that, still living in the same house but separate rooms *et al*. Can you blame me for dallying with fragrant, nubile ladies rather than someone in wellies and smelling of liquid fertiliser? Anyway, monogamy leaves a lot to be desired.

Patience was a word I couldn't utter at one time without squirming but given eternity I'm learning. Slowly, I'm having a revenge of sorts. I'm determined she's not going to enjoy my hard-earned money for very much longer… not that she spends a lot except on chipped bark, Growmore and peat. To wind her up, once, I pointed out that peat was over-used and bogs were in danger of environmental degradation – not that I cared greatly about Irish bogs. She gave me a withering look and slapped my dinner down on the table so hard the plate cracked. The offering, shepherd's pie, resembled a well trodden bog itself and my stomach revolted. Jean would have been better off taking note of 'Ready, Steady, Cook' than 'Gardener's World'.

John Innes was Jean's favourite of all the composts. I reckon that old John could retire comfortably to the South of France on what Jean purchased at garden centres every year. She needed it, she said, to fill the hideous pea-green ceramic pots she dotted around the lawn. They were big enough to conceal Ali Baba and a goodly selection of his henchmen. Talking of males, Jean doesn't seem to have had many men friends calling since my demise, except members of the green welly brigade and all they are concerned with is whose leeks or carrots are the biggest. She's no raving beauty herself, although I found her attractive once. She was tall and well rounded, but that was before she started double-digging and developed biceps like footballs. I did observe a somewhat tender moment with the fellow who came to prune the shrubs – a cut and slash merchant if ever there was one. There's no shade from the apple tree now.

Back to revenge. When I floated up out of the rose bed, next door's cat peed with fright all over Jean's rhubarb. The stalks are yellowing nicely. The same treatment effected the loss of the mint, thyme and rosemary, and I love the look on Jean's face as she scans the gardening books searching for a possible cause.

Dear Alan Titchmarsh
    Even though I lavish attention on my herbs and rhubarb, they are dying. Can you give me a reason?

What a laugh.

The Queen Elizabeth is blooming just above my right foot. Masquerade runs down my torso and I support a Danse du Feu on each arm and they're doing well. Bigger blooms and more fragrant than ever. Glorious, wafting on the air perfume is what I'm aiming for. Forty four years of excellent nourishment is feeding them better than the muck from Jean's green plastic bins. I'm putting all my effort into attracting the bees, swarms of them, from Jack Dawson's hives across the common, and it's paying off. The garden is humming with them, morning and night. Jean, you see, is allergic, so it's only a matter of time. Then maybe, just maybe, I'll come to terms with my lot and be able to rest in peace, or under Peace, I should say. That's the big cream one, with a tinge of pink…

A Bad Summer for Wasps

Sue Coffey

Eleftheria reached for the cake of soap on the kitchen windowsill and her fingers brushed against the leaves of the rose-scented geranium. At once, she breathed again the bittersweet aroma of lost summers. Digging her short, soil-filled nails into the soap's gritty texture she scrubbed hard at her cracked skin. This most special of meals would not be served on the kitchen table or outside under the pomegranate tree, but as was customary: in church.

Many years ago, in a different lifetime, when she and Yannis had married, their families and friends had showered them with pomegranate seeds after the ceremony. She had stood happily under the pattering of good wishes for love and fertility from the Holy Virgin and Aphrodite. Love had been hers from the first but fertility had taken so long that it seemed both God and gods were deaf to her prayers. But when, long, aching years later, the miracle happened and her beloved son had been placed in her arms he was so perfect, so beautiful, that she considered the anxious wait differently; as if it had been the only fitting payment for such a gift.

She dried her hands and set out the ingredients. Every grain of wheat, raisin, almond, sesame seed and drop of rose water was the very best that her orchard, field, store cupboard and purse could provide. All the care she had brought to preparing food for birthdays, Saints' days and Carnival over her long life shrivelled in comparison to her desire for this to be the best dish she had ever made. Nothing could be too good for her Andreas. *Their* Andreas. Yannis, working slowly and painstakingly and refusing all offers of help from much younger cousins had already cleaned the old pickup truck inside and out until the dented paintwork shone. Now he had gone to collect her sister's family. Everyone would cram in somehow, crumpling their Sunday best clothes.

On this day of all days her head seemed so full of the past that the buzzing seemed at first to be part of her darting thoughts. Then she realised that the tremulous hum emanated from a wasp that had made its way into the warm kitchen from the garden, seeking sanctuary perhaps from the first shadows of autumn. Like a frond of saffron the striped body vibrated in a spider's web that must have been as invisible to it as it had been to her until now. The trap had been spun and sprung high up between beam and wall.

Clambering onto a chair she reached up and brushed delicately at the web, freeing the wasp. She tried to fan it toward the open door but it stubbornly refused to leave. There was a time when she had killed wasps. But that was before Andreas, two years old and as sunny-tempered as a spring breeze, had shocked her one day by bursting into tears when she'd crushed the life from the troublesome intruders. She had returned to the kitchen – where she had left him enjoying his favourite dessert – to find wasps had arrived in numbers, attracted by the rose water she had sprinkled on the jewel-red flesh. He was holding his spoon up, entranced by the insects that quivered and fed there, so near to his precious, sticky lips.

14

'Look, Mama!'

His innocent joy had turned to incomprehension and grief as she dashed the spoon to the floor and set about squashing and breaking the magical creatures. And she, who hated to cause him a moment's anguish, had held his shuddering body close, kissed his dark curls and tried to explain how some pretty things hid a cruel sting. But she had promised she would not kill any more of them and he was soon laughing again. It was the beginning of his fascination with all things that flew.

Eleftheria poured a stream of cracked wheat into a bowl that had once belonged to Yannis's mother and mixed the coarse grain with just the right amount of water before adding it to the hot pan. She tasted a nut, holding the sweet sliver on her tongue, as she remembered how Andreas, on his chubby legs, had accompanied her up the hill above the harbour to where the almond trees grew. Every spring they picnicked under the pink blossom and after the first autumn rains he would help spread the sheets to catch the crop. Before her pregnancy she'd watched the other women up there, year after year, with ripening bellies, full cradles and noisy houses and hid her sadness behind genuine smiles and words of congratulation.

Until, in 1956, all of twenty-eight years ago now, her mother-in-law had suggested the couple visit relatives at Paphos. Yannis had only ever been there once before and she had never left the northern coast. Family: the visit had nothing and everything to do with that, because of course the fabled Monastery of Panayia Chrysorroyiatissa, Our Lady of the Golden Pomegranates, was there. They had gone there every day during that week and prayed for a child as never before – to the Holy Virgin who had suckled Christ on golden milk.

She smiled to herself, remembering, as she unscrewed the jar where she kept pieces of cinnamon bark and the smell of Easter and Christmas. Her breasts had been firm and high then and Yannis had loved to touch them during lovemaking. The golden pomegranate pendant still hung around her throat under her faded dress, as beautiful as the day he had bought it for her, only the skin it rested against had wrinkled and aged.

It was impossible to know whether Andreas had been conceived during an afternoon siesta that week or just after they had returned to Kyrenia. She hoped it was in his home town where he grew into such a fine young man. There was no doubt about one thing; Aphrodite had blessed her. Why else should she have craved the leathery-skinned six-sided fruit so much during those dreamy nine months? She'd helped harvest the pomegranates between that September and December. They kept well for a year but Yannis had joked that she'd eaten most of them herself long before then. It was true that she had picked out several of the pinkish-gold or brown varieties every day from where they had been hung to dry. Her mouth would be watering as she cut into the inner sections to plunder the transparent vesicles. Pregnancy suited her. She had sat there, fat and replete in the garden, lazy for the only time in her life, cupping the halved fruit in her hand and greedily spooning up the red juicy pulp and pointed seeds until the inner skin of the pouch lay clean and polished.

Another memory: mother and child tending the garden as the delicate scent of *Pyracantha* flowers and the rattling call of cicadas filled the air. To his delight she'd measured his growth year after year against the proud regiment of sunflowers standing guard along the sunniest wall. He always wished for more inches, while she would have stilled the relentless march of time if she could. She let him use an old, blunt knife to cut marjoram sprigs to flavour her cooking. She could see him now – hands outstretched to the marigold-dancing butterflies in the heat of the day or looking up as light faded and stealthy bats swooped to feed on complacent, sun-drunken insects.

Her deep reverie was broken by the sight of the wasps. Five of them were crawling over the pile of raisin stones stripping them of remaining shreds of flesh. She frowned. There had been summers when the swarms were numerous and in the battle for space they had tried to colonise wall cavities and roof spaces. If you didn't frustrate them quickly by destroying the foundations of the crumbly tier of brittle, yellow paper, a nest would be completed in weeks. Just one could easily house twenty thousand wasps. She must tell Yannis to check for signs of occupation.

1958 had been a bad summer for wasps. It had been a bad year all round. Of course, once Archbishop Makarios had rejected the British peace plan, trouble between the communities had been inevitable. But the scale of the violence took even the politicians by surprise. The old radio had crackled and hummed with bad news continually throughout those hot months. Forty people died that July, Greek and Turkish Cypriots, old shepherds and young children in the worst cases, but mostly young men. Why, she often wondered, had Aphrodite, goddess of love and beauty, chosen to give her love to capricious Ares? One gave fertility and life the other only war and death.

Sometimes, in a nightmare, she heard again the predatory howl of the air raid siren signalling the quarter to seven curfew. It would come as the horizon darkened, when the sun itself was scurrying for cover along with anyone careless enough to be outside. The screech of British jeeps and pounding of soldiers' boots would often follow as another search for EOKA members got under way. Spoon in hand in the kitchen, or tucking her son up in bed she would freeze, half-expecting the knocks, kicks and shouts that meant this was the night that her innocent husband would be taken away. But even worse than her fear of the British had been the new, creeping uncertainty of how much she dare trust her Muslim neighbours. Yannis had dragged Andreas's bed into their bedroom at that tense time and slept with an axe under his pillow.

Strange to think that just a couple of years later the whole neighbourhood was celebrating Independence. Everyone had been proud and happy. The children had clamoured for rides on their fathers' shoulders or danced down the winding streets alongside the band, waving their little white and gold national flags in time with the music. It was a day when being a Cypriot was all that mattered. The few aeroplanes the new republic could muster had droned overhead. Andreas, beside himself with excitement, had spread his arms and run around in puny imitation with the other small boys, Mehmet and Kerim, Michalis and Kypros, shouting: 'Look, Papa, look up there.'

The damp-washing smell of the *pourgouri* alerted her to the fact that it was almost cooked. Drawing the pan off the heat she covered it with a clean cloth. She waved her hand at the wasps hovering over the gelatinous pomegranate seeds, covered that bowl too and closed the door and window. In the small room the flowery scent from the uncapped bottle of rose water hung dense and hypnotic, like incense. How many times had she spooned tablespoons of the aromatic liquid into wedding cake mixture? She had always stirred it in after the butter and before the milk, giving the dough just the right amount of elasticity. Tray after tray of *loukoumia* she had made, shaping the little balls around the nut, or date, depending on the season, and then dusted them with snowy icing sugar once they were baked, dreaming as often as not of the day when she would bake it for her grandchildren.

She transferred the warm *pourgouri* into a large dish. It was the basic ingredient for *ressi*, the rich lamb delicacy. There was a saying that went 'a wedding without *ressi* is like winter without rain.' All the old customs had been observed during the preparation of it for *her* wedding feast. The wheat had been ground by the young people and washed in the village fountain up to seven times. But that was a very long time ago. Brides today wore white more often than red, the true colour of joy. Couples had even begun to contribute equally to their new home. Yannis, like his father and grandfather before him, had given only his limited education and fishing trade to the pact while her family had, in time-honoured fashion, provided a proper dowry: land, the materials to build a house and the furniture to fill it.

Mixing the almonds, currants, cinnamon and pomegranate seeds through the swollen, fragrant grain she hummed the old wedding verse she had sung as a young bride.

> *Branches of orange, lovely with flowers*
> *Seven are the bridesmaids who sew the bed*
> *Into the brides hall flew two nightingales*
> *They came to bring her English needles*

The mountains were the place to hear nightingales. Up in the villages where the air was cool and the trees kept their leaves into a late autumn. On their annual August holiday it had been difficult to get Andreas to lie still at night. Every time he began to settle the thrilling song would start up again, louder and sweeter, and he would be back at the window straining to catch sight of the shy choir. He would have liked to draw them. He had lots of sketches of the more extrovert birds, like swifts, curving through the sky or building their curious mud and spittle nests. He had even persuaded Yannis not to string lime nets between the trees in their orchard because he couldn't bear to hear the cries of the captured fruit thieves ripping themselves apart in an effort to free themselves.

Every spring and autumn they had come, thousands of migrating birds using Cyprus as a staging post between Europe and the Nile delta. Andreas had taught her to distinguish between the falcons, harriers and buzzards, the curlews, wheatears and shrike. The boy had never seemed intimidated by the sheer number wheeling over the farmland skies. He saw their numberless presence as a gift. She had always felt that the advantageous geographical position of the island was like the face of a beautiful woman: a mixed blessing. It had served its people well but also attracted an unhealthy amount of attention – Venetian, Egyptian, Ottoman, British…

She washed the pots before opening the glass cabinet and removing the engraved copper serving spoons that her grandfather had made. It was strange to see them ready for use instead of sharing pride of place with Andreas's photographs and school certificates. She had snatched up her most prized possessions in lieu of clothes and money the day she'd had to flee her home. And here they were, safe and sound, when so much else was gone.

With all prepared in the kitchen she stepped into the shuttered cool of the bedroom. Silk: only the finest material would do for a day like this. She slid the dress over her head and arranged the tiny golden orb so that it rested on her bosom. A cross was more usual perhaps, but church ceremony or not, the symbol of her greatest happiness was what she wanted to display for all the world to see on this anniversary.

Ten years ago, in 1974, it had happened: the Turkish Invasion of the island. And it had taken all this time for there to be formal confirmation that no prisoners had ever been taken. None of the fishermen out on the calm sea that terrible, beautiful July dawn, full of diving seabirds and jet fighters, would ever come home again.

Eleftheria had known the truth in her heart all along; ever since the first land-hungry troops had swarmed over the horizon colonising the coastal towns on route for the central plain. Every Christmas since, when Yannis had raised the defiant toast 'next year with my son,' in this refugee village, she had wept for her desperate husband and her lost homeland on the other side of the Kyrenia Mountains.

The familiar rusty horn sounding outside spurred her into reluctant action and she braced herself to pick up the heavy dish. The familiar ingredients lay at the heart of so many traditional meals cooked for family celebrations and in observance of the Greek Orthodox Calendar. But mixed and baked like this there was just one result: *kolliva*, the meal for the dead. Today, at Andreas's memorial service, dressed in deepest black, it was just possible that she might at last be able to shed a little of the unremitting ache with stinging tears.

She stepped out into the garden. Or perhaps that blessed release would only come on her return. When, like the ancient Greeks before her, she would kneel and plant marjoram in remembrance of a loved one. Unlike them she had no grave to use for her purpose. But she would place the cutting in the patch she had lovingly cleared this morning, just there, next to the pomegranate tree.

Jonesy's Place

Christine Hirst

At the the beginning of the story, a voice. Mine.
'Here it is,' I shout through the door as I kick off my boots, 'the last cabbage.'

No answer.

'Seb?' I shout, coming into the kitchen. 'Where are you? It's a beauty, come and see!'

No answer. Then I see the note. Sometimes, when something disturbing happens, I feel as though I am watching myself acting a part in a film I've seen before. Now I'm in that really sad part where there is a note propped up against the coffee pot on the table, an echoing silence as a voice calls out a name, a trembling hand as the note is read, a sob, a body sitting down casting a long shadow across the wall, two hands raised to the face and silent flowing tears. We've all seen it a dozen times, but this time it's happening to me.

> **Maggie,**
> *I have decided to go back to the City. I need to be with Madeleine. It won't affect the garden centre in any way. It's just a personal thing. Sebastian.*

It's just a personal thing, he says. I'm fed up with you he means, that's all. He is dumping me but keeping on the business. I have lived all the disasters of the world in my heart one way or another, and now here's one of my own. I feel myself falling down, down into the icy depths of the sea, drowning, drowning, calling out for help and getting no answer, no answer at all.

I don't know how long I sat there frozen in the heat of that summer day but I remember stumbling over to the tap and filling a glass of water and spilling it as I knocked the glass on the side of the sink. I slipped in and out of time. The past, the present, the future, all mixed up. I remember watching the water running down the doors beneath the sink and forming a pool on the tiled floor. I remember how the water distorted the pattern of the tiles as I peered at it, not drying it up. I remember going to the front door and looking at the empty space where he always parked his car. I remember looking in his closet, his drawers, his desk, and finding all of them empty and then saying out loud, in a burst of fury, 'Sebastian, you must have planned this. You must have sent me to the market to give yourself time to leave a note and go.'

I kicked his side of the bed. I ripped up the note and threw the pieces on the floor. Much later on I picked up the pieces. I would keep them, just to remind myself never to trust him or anybody else again.

Then I remember another great wave of anger overcoming me and I see myself running out of the house into the garden in my bare feet. I remember picking up an axe and chopping down his favourite lilac tree, then sobbing, 'Why, Seb? Why? Things are going so well. All right give up the garden centre, leave it, but don't give me up, don't leave me.'

But he had left me and Madeleine would be waiting for him in London.

I won't tell you about the next few weeks. If you really can't imagine it, then it's better not to try. At the end of a lot of fruitless phone calls and soul searching, I decided to carry on alone. Now I would know exactly where I was and no one could change my script without my consent. Then I met Jonesy.

Standing in the yard one day I heard the sound of a motor. At first I thought, I even shouted, 'Sebastian!' and ran to the drive only to see a small pickup backing up towards me.

'Hey there! Here's your compost,' shouted a voice. 'Where do you want it?'

I'd forgotten all about it. Rigid with disappointment I stood there for a moment unable to think.

'Hey there, where d'you want this lot then?' came the voice again.

'Oh, just there, by the shed,' I forced myself to answer and turned towards the cottage. I didn't want to see anybody but Seb.

'Hey, hey, hey,' said the voice. 'Hey, pleased to meet you, I'm Jonesy.'

A tall, capable-looking woman jumped out of the truck and came smiling towards me, hand outstretched. I shook it and managed a watery smile.

'Hello. I'm Maggie. The shed's just there.'

'Right,' she said, 'I'll unload, you put the kettle on.'

So I did. And the long and the short of it is that Jonesy moved in and became a sort of unofficial partner. A scene change I was happy with this time.

Jonesy was the hardest working person I have ever met. She appeared to thoroughly enjoy life and nothing seemed to worry her. Even when I broke my ankle and was only up to paperwork she did everything that needed doing. She made me laugh by telling me funny stories about things that had happened to her.

'My first and only marriage took me to Egypt,' she said one time, 'and there, just for a laugh, I went to belly dancing classes with some of the other Air Force wives.'

I nodded feeling a bit stunned, it didn't seem quite decent to me.

'Maggs, it was fun, we had some great times. I got really into it, the music and the history of it, you'd have loved it.'

Then she told me how her young husband, who every one called Jonesy, had been killed in a helicopter accident. She had no future there without him, so in the end she came back to Wales, took on his nickname to remember him by and got a job with a small haulage contractor. Then she met me.

I didn't know what to say, I kept thinking of the films. All the comedy and tragedy, all the fairy tale elements in real life…

'Hey,' she said, 'life is too short for misery; let me give you a little demonstration. I'll just get some music from my room.'

I heard her dash up the stairs and waited, feeling a bit

uneasy. This sort of thing made me nervous. But when she put some music on and began to move around the floor in perfect time to the unfamiliar but beautiful sounds I started to smile. Then I howled with laughter, and then I realised how good she was and burst into applause. I even started to copy her upper body movements from my chair and the two of us laughed until we cried, as only women can.

Dancing about became quite a regular thing in the evenings, when I got back on my feet, and I swear it made me stronger.

A sort of dream sequence followed, working, cooking, dancing and planning the future together. Jonesy and I both loved roses and decided to make a rose garden down on the flat land that lay next to the meadow. We would start it later in the year.

As we drew up the plans Jonesy sang the 'everything's coming up roses' song and we both got up and did a little dance. All those little scenes were shot through with the bright colours of happiness.

But it didn't last long. One Thursday, returning from market, we found Sebastian in the kitchen. And everything changed again.

'Sebastian!'

There he was, this tall handsome man smiling in the kitchen, and I promptly fell to pieces.

'Maggie,' he said.

That old film thing again. Was this happening? Was this handsome hero really holding me, plain old Maggs, in his arms?

'Hello there,' said Jonesy, finally breaking in, and smiling.

Drawing away, still trembling with shock I introduced them.

'Sebastian, this is Jonesy.'

'Who?' he asked, raising an eyebrow.

'My friend. She lives here now.' I shook as though I was guilty of something. I even apologised. Jonesy shook his hand and said, 'Hey,' looked at my face, smiled and left the room.

'I've come back,' he said coolly, confident of my affection.

I threw my arms round him again and cried. He patted me in a condescending sort of way and said, 'I'm back now; you've got nothing to worry about.'

'What about Madeleine?'

'She's got nothing to do with things now.'

Then I remembered Jonesy.

'But Jonesy lives here now. She works with me. I didn't think you were coming back.'

'Fine,' he said. 'As long as she knows her place.'

When a good-looking, classy man comes back to an unremarkable-looking stocky little lady she doesn't ask for too much. I left it at that.

Jonsey did know her place, or pretended she did to please me. She acted out the role that Sebastian gave her to perfection. But it wasn't her place; she and I both knew that. She was better than both Sebastian and me put together. She got up before we did and retired early. She didn't get in the way. She worked so hard she put us both to shame. Sebastian was polite to her and she deferred to him even when she knew he was wrong. Perhaps he saw her as a threat. Anyway, one day he told me to get rid of her.

Shocked, I tried to argue, to protect her. I put my arms round him and asked him to think again.

'Look,' he said patting me again, 'I've come into a fair bit of capital now. If we have to, we'll buy her off, set her up somewhere until she gets on her feet. But you must see that she can't live here for ever.'

He told me about his plans for development. He told me how much he was prepared to invest in our future and how he would pay off the bank loan on both the garden centre and the cottage. I protested at first and put up a feeble argument but, at last, as women do, I agreed.

I waited until the next morning before I told Jonesy. I worried about it all night, going over what I should say. When, finally, I did break it to her she didn't say much, she just looked at me. I felt as though I had committed a murder. I told her that too. She smiled, 'Oh, Maggs, don't worry about me. I'll be fine.' And then she started to cry.

Neither of us spoke for a short time and then she said, wiping her eyes, 'I won't really be leaving if I look for a place nearby. We can still be friends. It's the best solution really.' And we hugged each other for a long time.

'Dear Jonesy,' I said. 'Perhaps you could grow plants for the centre. For us. Just let me talk it over with Sebastian. I won't let you down, I promise.'

But I did let her down because Sebastian wouldn't hear of it.

ooooo

Another scene change. I felt really alienated from my life this time. I wasn't in control. That afternoon, in the kitchen, Sebastian very formally offered Jonesy a loan which she was to repay in five years. She declined gracefully, of course, and then she quietly packed her things and went. I can't tell you how dignified she was or how I felt. After that I watched the post for ages and jumped every time the phone rang but I didn't hear from her again.

For the next three years life went on very much as usual. I was still slightly out of touch with what was going on, but I got by. We were happy enough in some ways but we didn't actually laugh much. The colours had pretty well gone too and I settled for a monochrome existence. Part-time workers came and went and the business did well. My time with Jonesy seemed to fade into a dream but I found myself, in private moments, doing a little belly dancing and humming Jonesy's music. Then, one day, when I was at the market, I thought l caught sight of the back of her. Full of excitement, calling out her name, l ran to catch up. As I pushed and dodged the crowds it all swept over me, she was the best friend I'd ever had and I had let Sebastian try to buy her off and send her away. For a moment I hated him. I battled through the crowd but she wasn't there. Running, panting, sweating, calling out her name, you know the scene, and of course I lost her.

I went to the market every week after that, loitering by our favourite stalls, looking out for her, but she never came. Then on the fifth week I waited by the flower stall that we liked so much, which we wanted to fill with roses. Something made me turn my head and I saw a notice on the fence.

Learn to Belly Dance
Jonesy's Place, 10 Market Street. Opening Monday,
10ᵗʰ June 7.30 p.m.
Come Along.

I was so excited I went home without half the things I should have bought. Today was Thursday, three days and a few hours to wait. I danced about all over the place when Sebastian was out of sight, much to the amusement of other people who caught me unawares. Splashes of colour crept back into my life, more and more each day. On the evening of the 10ᵗʰ I washed up the supper things and plucked up courage to announce that l was going out. Alone.

'I'm just going into town to the, to the erm…library,' I said. 'I want to read about things.'

Sebastian peered at me over the top of the newspaper. 'What things?'

'Roses. I want to read about roses,' I said firmly.

'Why?' he asked, looking both surprised and dismissive at the same time.

'Because I do, that's all, they interest me. They always have.'

'That's the first I've heard of it, but if that's what you want, fine. Pick up some milk on the way,' he said, losing interest, and carried on reading the paper.

'Right,' I said and kissed the top of his head, 'see you,' and I grabbed my pumps and leotard, shut the door behind me and drove into town.

As I pounded down the street afraid of being late I saw her in front of me. 'Jonesy,' I shouted.

She turned round and smiled, 'Maggs.'

We ran into each others arms.

'I knew you'd come,' she said.

'Where is the class?' I gasped.

Her grin grew even broader. 'There is no class. It was just for you. But look. Look here at No. 10. This is my place now. My shop. I've just bought it. Come in.'

I went in. 'Jonesy's Place,' I said looking round, 'a flower shop.' And painted on a sign in red and gold italic script the old slogan, 'Everything's coming up roses.' Perfect.

'Jonesy! You remembered!'

'Of course I did. Do you like it?'

'I love it. Jonesy. It's the best thing.'

'Then tell Sebastian that you're moving in with me, because you are, aren't you?' and she did a little belly dance to emphasise the point.

'Yes,' I shouted, 'yes,' and we both danced around the shop laughing in a kaleidoscope of Technicolor®. The best scene of all.

Later that evening I slipped a note into the postbox at the cottage gate and in the blaze of the setting sun made the story my own again.

Sebastian,
I have gone back to town. I need to be with Jonesy. You can keep the market garden, but you'll have to get your own milk. Nothing personal. Maggie.

Windrush

Catherine Osborn

We're selling our dream-house, *Windrush*. And it won't be too soon. Why? I hear you ask. Listen. Have you ever lived in a place that seemed like Paradise? Then, suddenly it turns into Hell? It's happening at *Windrush*. That's why we can't wait to see the back of its trellised walls and latticed windows, why we long to escape the garden, with its winding paths, its lily pond and love seat behind the roses. Even Richard, my husband, agrees that we must go. Now that he knows what we know, and has seen what we've seen.

It's on the market for £800,000. One set of viewers, who came while we were away, fell in love with it and agreed the asking price. I'd feel guilty, if I wasn't so relieved. We'd have accepted less, a lot less to leave *Windrush*. But they, poor fools, what do they know of the place, or of the unspeakable strangers who drift in and out of the garden, even into the house, turning our dream into a nightmare?

We call them the *quarrellers*: We say it in a whisper because we are afraid, and don't want to be overheard.

It was our little girl, Jenny, who gave them that name, for it was she who first met them.

It was late July. We'd been here no more than a year when she came running into the kitchen from the garden. 'Mummy, who are those people sitting on the seat behind the rose bush?' she asked. 'Are they visitors?'

I wiped my hands on a kitchen towel and followed her into the garden.

'They're not very nice,' she whispered. 'They keep quarrelling, and the man made the lady cry. When I said "hullo" to them, they didn't answer. They didn't even look at me.'

As we hurried down the path I thought I heard snatches of conversation, but it might have been the rustle of leaves or the buzzing of insects, for when we reached the love-seat behind the rose bush, it was empty.

'They've gone,' Jenny said, frowning. She must have noticed my sceptical look for she said, defiantly, 'They *were* here. I didn't make it up. And the man was horrible. His voice was all growly. And he had a fuzzy beard and glasses, and a face just like this.' She screwed up her eyes and twisted her mouth into a scowl.

I didn't pay much attention. Tourists, I thought, unable to resist a peep at our garden. Or maybe Jenny imagined them. She's an only child, sometimes lonely and dreaming up companions. She'd done it before.

I forgot the incident until, a week later, she came running up the path once more, breathless with anxiety. 'Come quick, Mummy! Those *quarrellers* are here again, and that awful man is hitting the lady and hurting her. Make him stop!'

Once again I followed Jenny, but once again, there was no sign of them. I began to wonder if we should take her to a psychiatrist.

'Forget it,' Richard said. 'She's got a lively imagination, that's all... Probably seen something on TV that's sparked it off.'

I wasn't so sure. I kept a close eye on her after that. It's not too difficult now I've given up my job in town.

For a week we heard nothing more of the *quarrellers*. She's forgotten them, I thought. But one day, on opening the kitchen window – it was still very hot – I heard voices wafting in from the garden.

I looked out but could see nothing.

Jenny joined me at the window. 'It's the *quarrellers*,' she whispered. 'The man's being horrible to his wife again.'

She climbed onto the chair below the window and leaned out. 'Look, here they come.'

This time, I saw them. First, the woman – pale, willowy, with blonde, flyaway hair, emerging from behind the trees at the bottom of the garden. And she was running, as if for her life. Behind her appeared the shadowy figure of a man, fists clenched, mouth set in an ugly line. 'Helen, come back here!' he shouted. They were both coming up the pathway, towards the house. As they got closer, I could see that the man had a beard and black-rimmed glasses.

I could feel my blood pressure rising. Who were these people? How dare they invade our garden?

I opened the window wider. They had reached the patio now.

'Would you mind telling me what you're doing here?' I yelled. 'This happens to be private property.'

Neither gave me as much as a glance.

Instead, the woman turned her anxious face to the man behind her and gasped out, 'I was only going to see Sarah, George. Please don't hurt me.'

'Lying bitch! You were seeing *him* again, that fellow you met at the conference, the "*kind* gentleman", who gave you a lift home. And I thought that's all there was to it.' He spun her round to face him, 'But I was wrong, wasn't

I? You slept with the bastard!'

'No, George! No, you're mistaken.' She twisted away, eyes desperately seeking escape.

'You were *seen*, damn you!' He pulled her back by the shoulders and shook her. 'And you're still screwing around with him. I should have guessed the truth when I met him myself, and saw the way he looked at you.'

He flung her forward. She went sprawling, hitting her head on the patio.

I rushed to the kitchen door, ready to give him hell. 'You maniac! I'll report you to the police!'

I hurried down the steps. I'd invite the woman in, give her a cup of tea. Whatever had happened, she didn't deserve to be pushed around like that.

The patio was empty.

I stared, not believing. Where had they gone?

I ran through the gate leading to the outside lane. No sign of them. No sound even. Only the crackling of twigs as a squirrel bolted up a nearby tree and the buzz of a mosquito flying into my face.

I shook it off and stood, gazing into the emptiness, listening to the silence. Who *were* these people?

I longed to talk to Richard, but he was away on business. I didn't want to worry him.

Over the next few days, I kept Jenny close to me. We avoided the garden. The plants got watered, but that was all.

On the day before Richard's return, I went up to our bedroom to change the sheets. I paused outside the door, a prickle of fear starting up at the back of my neck. Someone was in there. I could hear the sounds of drawers being opened and shut. I was about to turn and run to the phone, when I heard a sob from inside. I made myself open the door.

And then I saw her, the same woman I had seen in the garden. She was alone and had a suitcase open on the bed. Her eyes darted about furtively as she hurried to fill it.

She appeared to be taking clothes from the wardrobe, but they were not *my* clothes. They were shirt-neck blouses and pleated skirts, things I never wear. Her forehead was creased with lines of nervousness, and from time to time she scurried to the window and peered out before continuing her task.

I stepped into the room. It was as if some unseen force was pushing me forward. 'Who are you?' I murmured. I moved closer and peered into the porcelain-like face.

She didn't answer, seemed not to see me.

I stretched out a hand to touch her. At the same moment, she and the suitcase on the bed blurred and melted into the blue and white stillness of the bedroom.

Shaking, I closed the door and went downstairs. My teeth were chattering in spite of the August heat. Had it been a hallucination? Or was I witnessing the unthinkable: the souls of dead people who might once have lived here?

I thanked heaven Richard was due back soon. The whole thing was making my head ache and I was beginning to jump at shadows.

The following day, while reading to Jenny in the sitting-room, I heard footsteps in the passage outside. I was ready to burst with relief.

'Richard?' I hurried into the passage.

There was no answer, but I heard a door slam.

Jenny ran past me towards the study. 'Daddy, daddy! You're back,' she yelled.

She pushed open the study door. I took her hand and followed her inside.

A shadow appeared to move in the corner. I froze. Jenny let out a cry. It was not Richard. It was the intruder, George.

I stood inside the door, transfixed, my daughter's hand clasped tightly in mine. I wanted to turn tail and run, pulling Jenny after me, but I felt paralysed, glued to the floor. I could only watch.

He was standing beside the writing desk, holding something in his hand. It looked like a pill bottle. He was fingering it, turning it round and round and muttering, 'So, she's leaving me for *him*? I'll see her in hell first.'

'It's that man, the *quarreller*,' Jenny murmured. 'Why is he here, Mummy?' She began to whimper and flatten herself against my waist. 'I don't like this house any more.' The whimper turned to a howl, the howl to an outburst of noisy sobs.

I came to myself then, and hurried her into the sitting-room. It had a lock on the door so I locked us in, knowing at the same time that locked doors are no protection from spirits. I prayed that my husband would return soon.

He arrived an hour later. I rushed into his arms, half-sobbing in relief, my words tumbling out in a torrent of incoherence. 'Oh, Richard, thank goodness you're back! We've got to leave this place. At once. There are ghosts. And one of them's really evil. Please, let's go away. Now.'

'Ssh!' He put his arm round me, but I could see his face darken. 'We're not moving, Kate,' he said, when I had calmed down. 'I'm not going through all that again.'

'But don't you understand? We can't cope any more. The place is haunted.' I broke into sobs again.

He shook me. 'That's nonsense, Kate! Stop it! Get a grip on yourself!'

I turned away, tight-lipped. He'd change his mind. I'd make him. If he didn't, I'd leave, and take Jenny with me. Perhaps then he'd come to his senses.

That night, as we sat in the kitchen, drinking tea and exchanging news, there was a noise outside the window. It was a strange, irregular sound, like something being dragged from the patio to the lawn.

'What was that?' I sat up, alert.

'What? I didn't hear anything.' He went back to his story, 'As I was saying …'

I tried to focus but I was too on edge, and too busy trying to make out another sound. It came again.

'Listen! Do you hear it?'

It sounded like a distant wail.

Richard paused. 'Cats,' he said, decisively. 'Cats from next door.'

'Please, I'm worried. Let's take a look.'

We went outside. A full moon lit up the garden. It looked calm, beautiful. We walked down the path towards the love seat, then on to the lily pond. Everything was still, silent. But as we neared the pond, we heard a choking, spluttering sound and a splash of water.

I started. Richard gripped my hand and we ran through the ornamental arch till we could see the pond before us. And there, beneath the moon, we saw a sight that made us both cry out: the heavy shape of a man bent over something that kicked and struggled at the side of the pond. As we got closer, we could see it was a woman. He was pinning her to the ground with his body and thrusting her head into the water. She was writhing and twitching. But by the time we reached the place, the twitching had stopped.

'What the hell?' Richard raced towards him. 'You bastard! Kate, get the police!'

My husband's a big man, sure of his strength. He made a grab for the killer.

'It's no use, Richard,' I called out, 'they're not real.'

Too late. Richard stretched out his hands and, as he did so, killer and victim began to fade away, until both had vanished into the night air.

Richard stood gaping at his empty hands, while I, beside him, tried to stop shuddering. What did this violence mean? Surely if it was something that had happened here, we would have heard about it?

Whatever it was, Richard changed his mind about staying. The next day, he put the house on the market. The day after, he arranged to take time off work, and we went to stay with friends and to search for a new house.

Today, we are back at *Windrush*, but only to see the estate agent. He is bringing our buyers with him. They are coming to measure up and decide where their furniture will go.

I'm feeling guilty again. Poor devils! But perhaps they won't be harassed by the *quarrellers* as we were. Maybe the spirits, or whatever they are, will leave them alone.

Richard reads the paper while we wait. Jenny is busy with her colouring book, sticking out her tongue as she concentrates. I potter, feeling calmer now. We all are. Two days ago, we saw a house we liked and put in an offer. It's been accepted.

The estate agent arrives early, our buyers close behind him.

I go to greet them with a smile. But my smile freezes. The man is thickset with a beard. He wears dark-rimmed glasses. The woman is pale, willowy, dressed in a pleated skirt.

'Let me introduce you to George and Helen Leech,' the estate agent says.

Richard steps forward, an arm outstretched in welcome. He has never met the pair in daylight, so there's no sign of alarm on his face. But I see something else there, a kind of joy, that only adds to my disquiet.

The woman flashes him a smile of recognition. 'So *you're* the vendor? She turns to her husband. 'George, this is the kind gentleman who gave me a lift from the conference that time. Isn't it amazing?'

My heart turns to a lump of ice.

She and Richard exchange glances, private, heavy with secrets.

George, her husband, purses his lips. 'Amazing indeed,' he grunts.

The words sound unreal as if coming from a distant planet, or a dream. I open my mouth to speak but can only gaze at the couple in silence.

Then Jenny looks up and gazes at them too. I see her face change, a frown appear between her eyes, and her mouth open in a silent scream.

Silver Bells and Cockleshells

Ella-Louise Gilbert

The last thing you think of when playing mother, cook, housekeeper and sister, is taking on the role of gardener as well.

When Mrs Jolly's frizzy white hair appeared, floating over the garden wall, Izzy and I were playing hide-and-seek in the knee-high grass – just perfect for disappearing into. Mrs Jolly dwelt in the shadows behind curtain-drawn windows. Sunlight was only allowed to touch her alabaster skin when she was overcome with the need to make a complaint.

'Could I have a word?' she bit. My stomach tumble-tossed. There's a lot you can acquire from just five words. I was transported to shifting from foot to foot, head bent in the headmaster's office. It was a sentence that reminded me of that thing I had come to despise most of all recently: responsibility.

'What's the problem?' I retorted, throwing back my shoulders, sticking out my chest like a peacock. I wasn't going to let her bully me into submission.

'I understand that you've had a lot to deal with recently, but it's been nine months now.'

Her mole-like eyes squinted in the sunlight. I willed her to crawl back into her underground tunnel and never, ever emerge again.

'I haven't said anything before,' she continued. 'I thought

you might come to the realisation yourself. Your garden is an overgrown, wild... chaos of weeds and whatnot. It's affecting the presentation of the houses around you. Mr Jolly is willing to trim your grass this weekend. I can give you tips on weeding and planting—'

'No thank you,' I interrupted. 'We're quite capable of doing it ourselves.' The words spat out more venomously than I'd intended and Mrs Jolly shrivelled away, stunned.

'If you can do it, I'm sure it can't be that hard,' I stated calmly with a smile. My feathers were fanned out in their full glory, and I paraded back indoors.

The day Mum died it snowed: buckets of icy tears, rolling down off the clouds, tumbling down my cheeks. I keep returning there; to that moment when nothing is normal – the cars won't start, the schools close and you are thrown out of routine into this blindingly white, unreal dream. Snowflakes stuck to my hair and caught in the creases of my furrowed brow, rendering me a wrinkly, grey-haired old lady before my time.

Mine were the first footprints to step out onto the smooth, fresh snow. My toes began to tingle with the cold. The chill travelled up through my body, freezing my feet, turning my legs to long icicles until my heart was cold and my mind was numb. So numb I couldn't feel anything anymore. A glacial wall had been placed in front of me and I was watching the world on the other side with a detached indifference. It was a window of frost turning everything a cold, blurry blue – a window to another universe, from which I had been cut off. My world would always be cold. I knew I had to break through to the other side where there was warmth and somehow take my brother and sister on the journey with me.

The day I learnt I'd won custody of Izzy and Ben was the day I saw my first grey hair in the mirror. I suppose most people would have plucked it from the root, but I've left it there. A permanent mark where the first fallen snowflakes had once marked my hair. A silver medal of my achievement.

All I knew about gardening was that the daffodils sprang up in time for St. David's day and that Mum's favourite – purple petals as velvety as cat's paws – emerged in the Spring. Recipes for special meals and the names of flowers had been discarded the moment they'd left Mum's lips. Now I wished I'd hung onto every word, concentrated so hard that I captured each moment like a photograph that I could see and smell forever.

The only evidence of life in that garden now was a nasty present from Mrs Jolly's cat. Perhaps I'd never get the garden to flourish like the green-fingered could, but all I needed was a little knowledge and a few pretty flowers in vibrant colours that I knew would have made Mum smile.

I scoured books in the library for pictures of what Mum's favourite flower could have been. I saw a flower with two black eyes and a comical moustache at its centre, and I smiled back at the face of a pansy. The book said pansies represented thoughts – strange, because I did *nothing but* think about Mum.

The lawnmower had been hibernating in the shed long enough to have grown numerous cobwebs. I entered, armed with feather duster and pounced on the sleeping machine. It purred into action, and then growled in delight as it fed on the tall, straw-like grass.

Ben sat carelessly in his window, dangling his feet over the ledge. He watched me with the usual embarrassment of a teenager over the hopeless struggles of their guardian. As my body vibrated with the power of the lawnmower, I suddenly became unsure of who had control – the machine or me?

'Ben!' I yelled through thunderous grumbles. 'As the man of the house, do you think you'd be able to tame this beast?'

Ben rolled his eyes and slothfully climbed back indoors. His gangly gorilla walk led him to the garden. He snatched the machine from me and grunted his agitation, much as a primate might push away his inferior. I felt useless. Leaning against the wall I melted into the creeping ivy and watched Ben zigzag his way across the lawn. Teeth clenched and brow furrowed, he vented his anger into every blade of grass. Nine months, and Ben hadn't cried once.

I caught Mrs Jolly smirking at the sight through her window. She hurriedly closed the curtains and shrank back into the dark. I picked up a pebble, turned it over in my hands and threw it onto her perfect lawn. Funny, how small things can make you feel so much better.

Where once we sunbathed, drank ice-cold lemonade and crowed of our fancy ideas for the future, now grew a muddle of entwined vines and brambles. Though spring was beginning, my mind was stuck in winter and

I imagined the garden a mess of sludgy snow, turned grey by many dirty shoes trampling all over it.

Everything looked weed-like to me. The only solution was to pull everything up – to start afresh. I spent Sunday morning tugging and wrenching in the garden. It was rather therapeutic – this throwing away of unwanted rubbish. My hands were those of a giant, controlling the smaller life. What got to live was up to me.

There were moments when I forgot; precious moments that were too thin and transparent to keep hold of. The tiniest of things were enough to remind me of her – the smell of roast potatoes or a mother dabbing ice cream from her toddler's chin. This time, it was a scruffy-haired lad carrying a bouquet of purple flowers past my window. In my haste to clear the garden, I'd completely forgotten to leave Mum's pansies alone. I felt as though I'd ripped away a part of her – cruelly torn the root of her memory from the ground.

Dinner was flavoured with my salty tears and Ben's bitter complaints of the food. Catering for different tastes was impossible. A chef has his staff to cook the various orders. I was painfully aware of being alone. I saw myself standing again on the clear blanket of snow. The footprints behind me led back to a windowless, long, dark tunnel. In front of me lay a never-ending field of perfectly clear snow that I was too afraid to step on. I traced my footsteps backwards.

Izzy was first to notice Mum's purple flowers had disappeared. Sometimes I'd forget just how perceptive a six year old could be. I waited for the tears to pour, but nothing came. Instead, she tilted her head like a curious puppy, and questioned, deadpan, 'Are we supposed to forget all about her?'

Ben pretended not to mind whether 'those pathetic flowers' had stayed or not. It sounds strange, but I longed to see him cry – just so as we'd have something in common.

Some days I just wasn't up to leaving the house. My area of safety stretched from the squeaky front gate to the broken shed at the back of the garden. I suppose it was a need to return to the bubble of protection that cocooned me when Mum was alive; the bubble that made everything seem less daunting.

I'd called in sick to work and was sitting in the garden hiding red, puffy eyes behind rose-tinted sunglasses; ironic as the world couldn't have been more dark and gloomy through my eyes. My garden was eerily bare. The grass looked yellow and thirsty for air, like the white wrinkly skin that's revealed when you peal back a plaster. Over the fence, Mr Jolly cleared his throat. On days like these, speaking to people outside your immediate pack is torture. I tiptoed toward the back door, hoping to dive inside before he got any words out.

'I have something for you here,' he twittered.

Damn, I thought. Not fast enough. As established, I was unacquainted with the properties of wild flowers, but Mr Jolly was easily identifiable as a weed. Puny and pathetic, he had an annoying tendency to turn up when you least wanted him. With a voice as thin as his frame, I imagined crushing him as he spoke, just as I had done the other weeds.

'We found this in the attic. It's a bit of an antique, but it'll do the job,' he said, and with scarecrow fingers passed a dusty book over the fence. I blew dust from the cover to reveal flaky, silver lettering, *Gardening for Beginners*. For a moment, I was an ungrateful child, disappointed by her birthday present. A weak cough reminded me of Mr Jolly's presence, and I forced out a thank you.

From the book I established that plants were exactly like kids. Each had different needs that had to be adhered to in order for them to flourish properly. But I had enough trouble organising two children, let alone managing a whole nursery.

The picture on the packet of Virginia stock showed the soft shades of a chalk painting, reminding me of a country house garden. I sprinkled the seeds onto the patch in front of the patio, so they'd be the first things seen when looking out of the kitchen window. I also brought snapdragons – mainly for their name. I envisioned fiery reds with pointed tongues emerging from the centre, ready to bite off your nose if you looked too closely. The vibrancy of autumn crocuses caught my eye and were also swiftly flung into the shopping basket. My garden was to be an artist's muse; a tribute to Monet, with cheerful dashes of pinks and purples.

Keeping up this new gardening ritual was as difficult as sticking to a diet. Not because I was distracted by more appealing things like sticky buns, but because Ben and Izzy came first. At times, I'd even forget to feed myself, never mind the flowers. Ben had end of term exams that he needed help with and Izzy's school play was coming up. Stupidly, I had agreed to make her sunflower costume. Finding green trousers and a green jumper for the stem was easy enough. Making the petals to wear around her head was a different story. When Ben threw the dining room door open, shouting that he'd never pass if I didn't help him, I was surrounded by a mess of bendy wire, glue and yellow crepe paper.

'Look, Ben,' I said, unruffled, 'I do intend to help you, but if you did more around the house, I'd have more time for things like that.'

'I do. Tidied my bed today,' he grumbled.

'Well...' I searched for the right words; encouraging, but not too praising, '...thank you,' I said. He smiled, remembered he was in a temper, dissolved the smile to a frown and stormed upstairs.

Izzy was perhaps the most wilted sunflower I'd ever seen. The petals refused to stay upright and kept curling inwards. On stage she was nothing more than a button-nose, bobbing behind the perfect-petalled, toothy-smiled sunflowers.

I needed far more time to prepare Ben for the exams. On his first exam day, he left for school an eggshell of emotions. I wished I could freeze the day; stop the world turning, just for a little, so I could lend an hour to Ben. The rotation was relentless though, and I was stuck fast to gravity.

After collecting Izzy from school, we both rushed home to nervously wait for Ben's return, hoping to see a smile as he walked through the gate – a sign his first exam had gone well. We watched with jealousy as hand in hand the mothers and their children passed our window. The hours passed, the sky turned grey and the air cooled – yet still Ben had not returned. I had terrible visions of him, frozen in a giant block of ice, his face screaming at me, shouting it was my fault he had failed. I phoned around his friends' houses, but all were convinced that Ben had returned home. With Izzy's hand in mine, we trawled the streets, shouting Ben's name frantically into the night sky. The only reply was the screeching of a fox cub, calling out to his mother.

We rushed home, set on calling the police, when my ears were distracted and irritated by the sound of our shed door banging in the wind. I went to slam it shut, ready to blame it for all my pain, my anger and all that was wrong with the cold, grey world. And there was Ben, cowering in the corner, uncontrollably weeping, howling like the fox cub for his mother.

'I couldn't h-h-hold it in anymore,' he sobbed. I went to hug him, but he pushed me away, screaming, 'I don't want anyone to see me!'

'It's alright,' I whispered, 'you're not a robot devoid of its emotion chip.'

Strings of saliva hung between his lips as Ben broke a half-smile. He looked up at me with doe-like eyes – just as he used to do when a toddler. Again I moved towards him, gently resting my hand on his shoulder before crouching down to sit next to him in the dark, musty shed. This time he yielded, resting his head on my shoulder, burying his face in my hair as he sobbed.

'They're gone – just like she's gone,' he sniffed.

'What's gone?' I said gently.

'The flowers. Her purple flowers. There's nothing of her left.'

ooooo

One very ordinary Saturday morning, I was struck by quite an extraordinary idea. I had just finished washing the dishes, when I heard a strange trumpeting sound coming from the garden. There was Izzy, in pink wellies and fairy dress, blowing raspberries through a watering can. Marching around the garden, she looked the happiest I'd seen her in a long while.

'I should send you to the circus – turning a garden tool into a musical instrument!' I laughed, picking her up and swinging her around. 'But here's a better thought, how would you like to use that can properly and water the flowers?'

'Just like Mary?' she giggled, clapping her hands together.

'Mary who?' I asked.

'You know, silly, Mary, Mary quite contrary.'

'That's right. You could plant things like her, too. There's an empty patch that could be yours. You're old enough to look after things now,' I winked.

I don't know why I hadn't come up with the idea before. I guess I thought, as the oldest, it was my responsibility to do everything. But not even Wonderwoman, not even Superman could do that. Not even Mum.

By allocating Ben and Izzy a patch each in the garden, I was teaching them responsibility, to reap what you sow and more importantly, the need to pull together, to fight as one against slugs, next door neighbours and the ever-spinning world.

Ben was less easy to convince. Flowers threatened any manly reputation he held amongst his fellow schoolmates. 'Herbs though,' he said, 'could be quite cool.' I was a little concerned about the suspicious looking herbs Ben started growing in the attic, but nosey neighbours saw nothing more than chives and parsley over the garden wall. And, of course, there was rosemary – for remembrance, he knew that from his exams.

Izzy picked out cornflowers. She said they were the sorts of flowers Mum would have liked. She danced around the garden, showering the cornflower seeds like fairy dust.

I poured myself a glass of ice-cold lemonade and lazed back in a patio chair. Finally the frost had melted; my mind had thawed and woken up in spring. Looking around the garden, I could see that many more little green shoots had begun to break through the soil. Tiny buds were visible on the older ones. Those buds felt like a message; a sign I didn't know I'd been waiting for until then – confirmation that I was doing something right.

One bud was larger than the others. Its presence was mysterious and exciting as I couldn't remember planting it. I squinted to see what it could be. Wrapped in the bud was a squirt of colour – a particular purple that filled my eyes with tears.

Turns out, some things you thought were gone forever are still there. Look hard enough and you might find them; buried beneath the snow.

Rosemary and Rue

Sue Anderson

On a hill overlooking the river is a garden. I spend quite a bit of time there, balancing the red and the pink, the blue and the gold. I still don't remember the names of most of the plants. But that's all right. People do some of that for me. I met one of them in town a few months ago; she came at me out of the blue.

'Margery! Margery Williams!' She was thin and tall, dressed in a long purple coat, with shoes that couldn't possibly be from this century. She looked familiar, but I didn't realise she was addressing me: I haven't been Margery Williams for many years.

'Margery, I'm talking to you, dear.' A commanding voice. One to call you back from your daydreams, to make you straighten up and put your shoulders back.

'Oh gosh!' The phrase isn't one I normally use. We said it all the time in school though. And that's appropriate, because now I remember. The last time I saw this person she was standing in an oak-panelled hall, holding her retirement present: a set of gleaming, garden tools.

'Thank you so very much. I can honestly say I've enjoyed every minute of my time here. And I promise to come back and see you all.'

'Miss Byrne. How are you?'

She nods, impatiently, 'Oh, well, well, well. Enough to tell a hawk from a handsaw. What on earth are you doing here?'

She's staring at me. The grey eyes are still sharp. The tall figure is a little stooped, but it's not surprising: she must be eighty-five if she's a day. But she looks much the same, and she remembers me, in spite of my spreading waistline and the tinted hair. And now I'm fourteen again.

'I live here, Miss B.'

'How peculiar. So do I. I'm in town with the Garden Society. Lot of old fogeys. No idea where they are. Come and have a cup of tea.' She looks round vaguely and spots a little café. 'There it is. I always go there. The staff know me.'

They don't seem to, but it doesn't bother her. She selects a table in the window and orders a pot of tea. 'And cake please. Carrot cake. For two.' The waitress goes off and I'm left staring at the lined face, the wispy hair pulled back in a bun, the bright purple scarf. When I am old I shall wear purple.

Our class gave her a special leaving present – a plant. I was class captain and I got the final choice. I knew nothing at all about plants, but I knew it had to be purple.

Miss Byrne was our English teacher, one of the old school, the ones who made you learn things by heart and copy things out. We all hated her at first but over the months, as she softened up, showed her sense of humour, we grew to love her. We learned to see the twinkle in her eye, and enjoy her wrath when it fell on unsuspecting outsiders. Even now, I can remember chunks of poetry and lines from *Macbeth* and *Hamlet*. It's been a comfort. And as she thawed, she let us in on another secret: her passion for gardens.

The waitress comes and I pour the tea. Miss B's hands

seem too frail and bony to manage the heavy pot. She gulps greedily and starts on her cake, scooping up stray crumbs as she goes. There is no polite conversation, thank goodness. No questions about husband and family. Just silence, while Miss Byrne eats her cake.

'You're still gardening, then?' I say, eventually.

She looks up. 'Oh, of course. I'm just selecting some spring bulbs. We had a magnificent show last year. And I'm planning a new herb garden. Rosemary and rue and all that.'

A line of Shakespeare prickles in my head. 'Rue… Herb o' grace o' Sundays.'

'Well done.' She smiles at me, and another fragment pops up.

'And rosemary, that's for remembrance.' I always loved poor Ophelia. I used to fantasise about her making love to Hamlet, charming him out of his melancholy. Not that she could have of course. Probably not.

Miss Byrne is still talking about plants. All the long Latin names that I don't know. Finally she says, 'Do you have a garden, dear?'

'Yes. Not a huge one, but it's lovely. My husband…'

There is a fresh silence while I frame the next sentence. 'Takes care of it?' 'Used to take care of it?' I settle for, 'My husband's always been a great one for plants.' Which is true. There was a time when he read gardening books in bed. He could tell you the Latin name and the growing conditions for anything you cared to mention.

'Don't know how you do it, love,' I'd say. And he'd say, 'If you're interested, it sticks in your mind.'

'Sweet bells jangled, harsh and out of tune.'

'I beg your pardon, dear?' She's raising her eyebrows,

and looking stern, as if I haven't done my homework.

'Sorry. I was just thinking how clever you are to remember all the names. I can't get them into my head.'

'Well you should take the trouble to learn.'

'I know. I always meant to. But I don't have much time these days. I do a lot of…sewing.' (And how much have I done lately?) 'I like making patchwork quilts. You know, you always said I had an eye for colour.'

'Did I, dear?' her grey eyes are suddenly cloudy. She looks puzzled. I change the subject. 'Tell me more about your garden, Miss Byrne. Is it nearby?'

'Not too far,' she gestures vaguely. 'Somewhere out of town. On a hillside.'

'That must be lovely. I'd like to see it.'

'You should come for the daffodils. I always—'

'Miss Byrne!' A stout woman in a flowery hat is pushing her way between the tables. 'We've been looking all over for you.' She grabs Miss B by the arm, and I get up to protest, but my old teacher struggles to her feet and allows herself to be tugged towards the door. The woman is chivvying her: 'Come along. Can't keep the driver waiting. He'll be ever so cross.'

Miss Byrne is getting away. I can't allow this; I don't want to lose her. I push my way between the tables. 'Excuse me. I just need a word.'

'What is it?' The woman glares at me, but I'm not giving in.

'I just need Miss Byrne's address. I haven't seen her for years and—'

'It's Cheyne House. It's about two miles out of town. Just go south, along the river. You can't miss it. But be sure to ring first. The number's in the book.' And they're off, heading out of the door and down the street, where a minibus is revving its engine on a double yellow line. I watch the woman help Miss Byrne into the back and they're gone in a puff of exhaust.

Someone is standing behind me. It's a waitress. I realise what she must be thinking, and hastily pull out my purse. 'Sorry, I wasn't trying to… How much do I owe you?' She leads me to the cash desk and I pay the bill, leaving a large tip in the box marked 'Staff', but I can still feel her disapproving look as I leave the café. It's that horrible woman's fault. How dare she barge in like that and spoil our conversation?

On the way back to the car, I mull it over. Didn't think much to that Garden Society woman. She should show a bit more respect to the president. It's downright rude to boss somebody around like that, even if they are elderly. I'm still thinking about it as I drive home. I even forget the usual sinking feeling as I turn the corner.

The house isn't grand but it's nice enough. The garden still looks good, although it's been neglected lately. We've had a long, hard winter and now spring has come the weeds are already starting to grow. Things rank and gross in nature. Another bit of the bard. Another job for me.

My keys have wriggled to the bottom of my bag. No good expecting anybody to answer the doorbell. I fish around until I find them and let myself in.

Weeks later, worn and stressed from the effort of filling in endless forms and answering infinite stupid questions, I acquire a helper: a young lady who likes jigsaws and can give me a couple of hours of valuable time. I leave her talking to my husband and head for the great outdoors. It's a lovely spring morning. The sky is blue and the birds are singing. I have three whole hours. What shall I do? The answer comes straight away.

A mile down the road I suddenly remember I was supposed to ring. Never mind, if Miss B's out I can still get a glimpse of the garden.

The bossy woman was right: it is easy to find. The sign is in gold letters on a black board: 'Cheyne House. Retirement Home.' I should have guessed.

A gravelled drive snakes away up the hill and disappears between tall trees. Oh well, in for a penny. I follow it, hearing the car's engine protest at the pull. It really is steep. No elderly person could possibly walk up here. They'll all be stuck, at the mercy of minibus drivers. Still, at least Miss Byrne has the chance to keep up with her hobby. I'm looking forward to seeing her herb garden.

Coming out from the trees, the drive sweeps round and there is a wonderful view. Far below, the river winds between plaited hills in all shades of green. Daffodils are lined up along the edge of the well-kept lawn, which still shows great patches of gold and purple crocuses, like a huge quilt.

The house is pretty too, old brick, with smart white paintwork. I stop the car and get out.

The air is different up here. It seems to shine. Misty sunlight is diffused in it and fills your lungs, making you feel lighter. I go up the steps to the big oak door and ring the bell. The bossy woman opens it. She's frowning.

'I've come to see Miss Byrne.'

'I'm sorry...' She peers at me. 'Oh it's you. Did I mention you had to ring?'

Flaming cheek. What's it got to do with her? But I'm polite. 'I'm sorry. Were you having a meeting?'

'Pardon?'

'The Garden Society. Miss B mentioned she was president.'

A rather unattractive smile appears. 'Oh no, dear. That was some years ago. She lived up north, I believe. Oh dear no. I'm the owner.'

'Sorry?'

'I own the house. Miss Byrne is one of our old people. We provide expert care. That's our mission statement.'

Now, suddenly, I become aware of my immediate surroundings. There is a walking frame in the corner of the hall. And the smell of disinfectant isn't quite masked by the big bowl of lilies on the table. I hate lilies.

'Oh well,' says the woman. 'As you're here, you'd better come up. Be careful of the laundry.' It's stacked in piles along the endless corridor, with its identical green doors. The woman taps on one and opens it without waiting for an answer. Miss B is sitting in a chair by the window. She turns to look at me and my heart sinks. I've seen that stare so many times.

And once again, I have to identify myself. Facts acquired. Language. Concepts.

'It's me, Miss Byrne. Margery.' She doesn't answer. She's eating a biscuit and the crumbs are on her chin.

'I've come to see the garden.'

There is a sudden change. The eyes brighten. The face becomes animated. 'Oh that's wonderful. Can I go with her?' She's looking up at the stout woman, who's looking at me.

'You'll have to help her. She falls quite often.'

61

'Of course.'

'I'll get her things. She'll need wrapping up.'

So I take off Miss Byrne's slippers and put on her black shoes. And I help her into her purple coat. I'm good at this sort of thing: I've had practice. We take the service lift down, with the laundry, and are let out of the back door where the steps are not so high. I hold out my arm and Miss Byrne grasps it firmly with both hands.

'Can we see the hellebores?' she asks.

'I'm sorry. I don't know which ones they are.'

'I'll show you. They're under the trees over there.' We set off across the smooth lawn, and as we go, the years roll back, and she becomes the leader. 'See those anemones, dear? The purple ones, just coming through. I planted them. And the *Forsythia* over there. I brought cuttings when I came here and now it's everywhere.'

I spot a big, greyish green plant with delicate blue flowers like tiny orchids. 'What's that, Miss Byrne?'

'*Rosmarinus officinalis.* Rosemary,' she says, seeing my puzzled face.

'Rosemary. That's for remembrance,' I say and she gives me a smile, then frowns. 'There is no rue though. There ought to be rue. A bitter plant, but it has healing power.'

'Men call it herb o' grace o' Sundays. Of course. I'll bring you some.' I can buy a pot. Or is it the sort of thing that grows from seed? I'll ask— No I won't. I push the thought from my mind and we carry on round the garden. Miss Byrne names all the plants, things I barely recognise. Common names and Latin terms dance off her tongue, and she is a teacher again.

A bell rings in the house. Lunchtime. I look at my watch and realise with a shock that I only have half an hour to get back. 'Miss Byrne, I'm really sorry, but I must go.'

She doesn't seem to mind. 'Yes, dear. Come again. I'll break out the sherry next time. Oh, wait, I have a little gift for you.' She bends down and pulls a sprig off one of the plants. Hands it to me solemnly: my leaving present.

In the hall the thorny woman is hovering. I ignore her. 'Thank you so much,' I say to Miss Byrne, 'I've enjoyed every minute of my time here. And I promise to come back and see you.'

'That will be nice,' she says. 'What did you say your name was, dear?'

I'm late back but the girl is good about it. I wave her goodbye and turn to my husband. He's still sitting in the chair at the table, staring at the jigsaw. He doesn't seem to know what to do next. I go over and put a piece in for him and he smiles up at me.

It started quite suddenly. He kept forgetting things, and we'd laugh about it and say we were getting old. But we weren't really old, we thought. We still had plenty of time to enjoy the things we loved. More time, now he was retiring. Years and years.

Only it didn't turn out that way. The symptoms got worse and worse, and eventually, after agonising weeks, the verdict came like a curse. 'I'm sorry, Mrs Sharp. I'm afraid your husband…'

It seemed like the end of the world. Still does. I sigh and take off my coat. Something falls out of the pocket and I bend to pick it up. It's Miss Byrne's gift. The sprig of—

'Rosemary,' he says, staring at the bit of green in my hand. '*Rosmarinus officinalis*. Flowers from March to May in the south. Grows in dry, well-drained soil. Easy to propagate from cuttings. Has medicinal uses.'

'Medicinal uses,' I say, 'like rue. Do you know about rue?'

'*Ruta graveolens*. Bitter herb. Said to ward off evil.'

The bitter sweet herb of grace. I smile at him. 'You know so much about plants, love. I was just thinking, there's a lot of work to do in the garden. Will you help me?'

He smiles and nods. I know he will.

Gift

Vivien Kelly

I knew which tree it was, the place where they had buried her ashes: a mature sessile oak, just outside their home at the edge of the wood. I often walked there: the rough paths and struggling green a soft contrast to the clipped, verdant lawns that corralled my own house.

There was no plaque, but within a week of the service the bereaved woodsman was putting a light fence around the oak – to deter the squirrels, I supposed, or maybe just to mark it as special. I called my dogs away from its seductive scents. He nodded a brief hello and went back to hammering the post, his eldest boy holding it in place, the youngest watching, wide-eyed.

For Easter the boys pinned pictures of eggs and bunnies on the trunk of the tree – *look Mummy, see what I made*. The dogs had learned to pay no attention by this point, but my daughter, Clara, ran to tear off the pretty things. He brushed my apology away with a polite word. When I got home I found George, my husband, poisoning the burgeoning dandelions – *got to keep them down, best to start now*. The next time I saw the woodsman by the tree I stopped to say hello.

May bank holiday found George and me at the garden centre. Clara treasures pink carnations, I love *Clematis*, we came home with *Hostas*: fat green blobs. *They'll be architectural*. Blossom carpeted the paths of the woods. My walks took me past the oak more often now and if I saw the woodsman there we exchanged greetings and talked about our days. A delicate daisy chain made a may-queen crown for the tree's lowest branch. *My youngest – he thinks I don't know – he's embarrassed at doing it.* A wry sadness lifted the corners of his mouth. A sudden picture in my mind of planting a kiss there, a tingle of shock: I smiled back.

Handmade cards appeared in June: what was probably an elephant balancing on a ball, a bright yellow daisy-like flower. He caught my hidden look and explained, *It is – was – my wife's birthday.* The past tense landed heavily between us. The daily exchanges shortened for a while. I walked the same route every morning, always pausing at the tree, persisting, until the precious interaction grew again like the acorns. George bought an edge trimmer for our anniversary.

The summer break was too long. I came back to find postcards and photos huddled around the roots, quickly soaked by September rain. Neither of us seemed to have had a good time on holiday *but the kids' happiness is what counts.* George declared the garden to have gone wild and set about taming it with fork and hoe. I tried to tell him that it needed to be allowed to grow but he didn't listen.

Halloween saw spooky mobiles swinging from the branches – monsters and witches. My daughter screamed in delighted terror. His sons thanked me solemnly for the pumpkin. Later, he explained that the squirrels trashed it on the first night, and seemed relieved when I laughed. *They put a candle in it,* he said, *but even that got eaten.* Fallen leaves lay unswept behind the fence. George and I weren't talking, though I was not sure he had noticed.

Bonfire night found us all at the park for the firework display. Oohs and aahs and toffee apples, walking home in the dark, torchlight signalling our way when it wasn't being used by the boys to make their faces look ghostlike and thrillingly scary. The perfect night. George had had to stay late at work. He was doing that a lot.

Christmas decorations glowed in the weak sunlight, odd on a leafless tree. *Pity he didn't choose an evergreen,* people said, as if an oak wasn't good enough. Defiant lights embracing the trunk flickered and failed, flickered and shone again. We didn't need to say much to each other now; just being together by the tree was enough. When we did talk it was usually about the kids. *Christmas will be the hardest time for the boys.* Clara and I took more care in buying their presents than we did with George's.

We both had family over for New Year so didn't get many chances to meet. My mother-in-law went on and on as usual – *a lovely woman like that in the prime of her life, cancer, wasn't it? That poor man, those poor lost boys.* It took all my strength not to scream – a normal holiday visit.

January snows bent the tallest branch until it split off from the tree but he didn't cut it for kindling. *Better for the wildlife to leave it.* Our daily connection was the only thing in my day I looked forward to – the dogs took the path to his house automatically now. I knew that soon he would invite me in and I was content to wait, leaving all the unspoken things between us until then. Poor George swept the driveway every morning only to have it snow again in the evening. I brought out a cup of cocoa. *You seem cheery, I mean…it's nice to see you smile.*

On the second of February I slipped on a patch of ice right by the tree and the woodsman reached out to help me up – the first time we had touched. *Ice on St Bride's day. Winter will be here for a good while yet.* I shivered and gripped his arm, the ground beneath my feet uncertain. He steered me onto the edge of the path without looking into my face.

It was two weeks before I got the courage to walk that route again. George and Clara grew spiteful and peevish: *you're no fun any more, mummy; I see the good mood didn't last long.* I told myself the weather was too harsh, the ground too rough, but a lonely, pale ray of sunshine, the promise of spring pulled me out there one more time.

Approaching the house I could hear my heart beating loudly against my chest. I couldn't see him; he wasn't there. I would stand by the tree a moment or two and then walk on. I would do this every day and eventually he would come out and everything would be back to how it was.

My attention was snared by a crimson slash at the foot of the tree: a dozen red roses. I stood frozen in my arctic fleece. There was no card, no vase, the long, unbound stems lay as they had been reverently placed, crystal drops of melted snow jewelled the soft, dark petals. These were not children's gifts to a fading memory; they were an unashamed, public testament to passion and loss.

I felt it like a blow: he had given her a lover's gift – a sensuous, wound-red, open-heart valentine. I don't know which was more shocking: the nakedness of the gesture or how it tore away my own flimsy illusions.

Disappointed, the dogs trailed behind me as I fled back home. George was waiting for me. *We need to talk.* When, finally, I left the house again, it wasn't to walk in the woods...

Monstera Deliciosa

PennyAnne Windsor

They mock me. They hurl insults at me. Make patronising remarks. Fiddle with my private parts. Believe me, I know all about their so-called 'compassion'. I've seen the leaflets. I can see them now!

Children…Disabled…Single parents…Retired… Dyslexia…Alzheimer's… loads of feel-good money. Me? I might as well be in the rainforests of Mexico! Which is, after all, where I should be. Meanwhile, Tesco's. 'Swansea,' someone said. Can't *see* anything myself. No Mexico. No swans.

They do such personal things to you in Tesco's, Swan*see*. I don't know why it's allowed. All this fuss about *abuse*. I could tell them something about *abuse*. 'Dried up,' one woman says, spilling out of her trousers like an overstuffed cushion, face as red as a baby's bum with nappy rash.

'Oh,' you say, 'and how would you know about a baby's bum?' Well, I've been in Tesco's *a long time*. Plenty of babies to observe, especially when they move me to the changing room to make a space for mince pies or fireworks. And I have, of course, *tribal memories*. I can remember being large and tall and lush and glorious. Painting the jungle red! Talking about red, one man came in last Saturday, standard kind of bloke for this part of the world, so I've gathered from my observations. Short, wide, loud, beery… Not such a bad sort. Just out of his depth with *thinking* and all that sort of thing.

Big hands. A brickie probably. Used to play rugby. Off to watch the match. I was in agony! The way he squeezed. Sadomasochism, that's what I call it. Nobody, just nobody, has the right to do that.

'Past its sell by date,' he said. Everybody could hear, but he didn't care a damn. 'Well, mate,' I thought, 'so are you. So much as kick a rugby ball now and you'll be gutted.'

And this 'it' business. How demeaning. It! I am, of course, of the female gender. What else? I am not *anon*. I have a name, a gender, a heritage, a family, a future... Well, one hopes so... Past one's sell by date, indeed!

Well, a sort of future does arrive. It starts inauspiciously. A young girl pulls some of my aerial roots, pulls hard, mind you – not just a tweak or a tickle. 'It's like the end of a skipping rope,' she remarks to no one in particular. Well, I could see where that was going! But, before I could say 'Swiss cheese', a woman – presumably the child's mother – plonks me in a trolley with a pound of Granny Smith's and four mini yoghurts (reduced).

'That'll do for the windowsill,' she says.

'Do!' 'Windowsill?' The lack of grace! The absence of finesse! The sheer ignorance when confronted with such potential! I nearly give up there and then, root-bound and parched as I am. Give up the battle for life, let alone for any dignity...

The windowsill proves somewhat better than I had anticipated, though most situations are better than Tesco's. (I understand Tesco's is taking over the world – which doesn't bode well for my Mexican relations.) On the windowsill I have a clear view of children playing under the lamp post at the end of the front garden. At least, not so much playing as *congregating*. I think 'fucking' now permeates my root system like the lettering on a piece of seaside rock the girl child put beside me one day. Disgustingly pink and sticky – and *sucked*. However, water is provided and when I uncurl a pale, elegant, new leaf (a superb specimen, though I say so myself), well, a bigger pot is provided. After that, I must admit, I do try to leave my traumatic Tesco's experiences behind in the small pot that has been given over to one of those stupid pink begonias that spread like pimples in summer.

In the new pot I throw my inhibitions into the strong west wind and they are probably all over the Americas by now. I bud and sprout, thrust and twirl, round and upwards and outwards. By September, I reach the ceiling. Fuck elegance; fuck dignity! This is *fun*!

But such is life… Fun, as well as pride, is followed by a fall from favour. I know from the hubbub around me: the continual bumps and thumps, the smell of empty corners, that we are going on a journey. Of course, I dream Mexico, dream friends and relations, dream up a whole new identity free from that hideous name she's given me, *Frederica*. I mean it's not really a name at all, merely a female diminutive of Frederick. And who is Frederick? I imagine some pompous prick (another word I have learnt from evenings under the lamp post) – on the Managing Board of Tesco, lots of ready money, bags of jargon and as much class as Japanese knotweed. Spreads like wildfire and kills everything in its way! Swiss cheese plant is bad enough, but Frederica? Does she *know* – does anyone know – my rightful name is *Monstera deliciosa*. Consider that! It is, however, with some glee that I can tell you that it took three men to move me – pot, stakes and all. I cling to the walls and ceiling as long as I possibly can. Home, after all, is home, even if not up to my expectations. I hear one of the men say, 'Can't guarantee we won't break a branch or two, love. Not used to one this size.'

Then there is a snap as one of my lower branches cracks on the bottom of a cold metal surface and my aerials are tied – *tied* – with string. Worse is to come. No soft sunlight here, filtering through the trees; no lush heat, no heavy, warm rain. Utter exposure. With my aerials tied and rolling on my side, I am *mortified*.

It is difficult, though, to be *mortified* by one's exposure when one is literally mortified by a freezing wind. It blows from the sky, from the sides of the road, from under the very wheels. And that's how I arrive, I am lodged in the corner of a large kitchen where I am at least upright. But that's all. It's been too much. My glorious upper and lower branches broken, my beautiful split umbrella leaves torn. Worse than torn, in some cases: shredded. Soil spilt from my pot. Damaged roots. Need I go on?

All this matters. Of course. Such injuries always do. To be honest, however, although all this has made me feel a fool, a weakling, a coward – it's the cold that has really ended it all. I cannot feed from the air or drink water from my depleted soil. If I wasn't propped up in this rather ungainly fashion, between the table and the curtain rail, I would fall splayed horizontally across the kitchen floor. Just shows… As long as good old *Frederica* is vertical and hasn't actually died, then she's ok. Well, this time she is *not* ok. This time she's fucking freezing to death.

I suppose I lost consciousness. Strange dreams… Tesco's taking over the jungle… All my relatives in pots, so small that their roots screamed… Shouting in the last house on the windowsill… A man's voice, cigarettes stubbed out in my pot from a hand stinking with rage… The lady-woman and girl-child crying soft lost cries that went on and on through the night, long after the lamp post congregation had gone home…

Now I know a bit about *abuse* from my experiences in Tesco's, which, as you know, is where I began this reminiscence. It has a strange smell, like plant stems and leaves rotting in a jar. And that's the smell I smelled on the windowsill.

When I come round there are curtains on the rail. Warm velvet. My aerials begin to twitch at the thought of rooting in them, on the way up to another ceiling. This one's quite high. Quite a challenge. And my plain brown pot has been swapped for a large, blue, ceramic job – with a picture of leaves on one side. As though I need a picture of leaves! Nevertheless, it is a comfortable pot, roomy and really quite handsome. And a new layer of soil has been added, rich with sun and rain… I could almost forget my resolution to die!

Then I hear the lady-woman and the girl-child laugh and, completely ignoring the dreadful name she has given me, and the freezing journey I have recently undergone, I reach out one perfect closed, rolled leaf. Just to test the air.

I haven't heard them laugh for months. I look up at the high ceiling and that dreadful draught slips into my past with the terrible episode at Tesco's. After all, I'm fit and beautiful – in fact *bloody gorgeous* – and with my heritage… a bit of budding and climbing, thrusting and twirling…I could reach that ceiling, fill this room. *Monstera deliciosa* takes over the world!

Fuck it (if you'll excuse the lamp post language)! This could be fun.

High Noon

Hilary Bowers

It must be hormonal, Jenny decided, as yet again she positioned herself between the two protagonists. Either that or downright mutual loathing.

Dot and Maisy, the 'Little and Large' of Edenfield Hospice Charity Shop, and its backbone. Without them, keeping the shop open would be impossible, and at that moment they seemed hell-bent on murdering each other.

The problem was that they both liked dressing the window, but Maisy, the morning 'girl', always got first crack at it. Poor Dot, who took over from Maisy at one, faced with a *fait accompli*, would spend the afternoon muttering about people who should know better, acting like big kids.

Or rather, she had until recently; four weeks ago to be exact. That day, the sight of Maisy's latest effort – two broom handles acting as mannequins, bedecked in animal-print dresses and scarves, surrounded by prides of furry lions, tigers and zebras, plus a few monkeys, a pink elephant and an unsettlingly life-like snake thrown in for good measure – had tipped Dot over the edge. Ignoring Jenny's pleas to calm down, Dot had thrown the plush zoo back into the almost empty wicker basket, reserved for children's soft toys, that Maisy had raided for her display, and proceeded to fill the bottom of the window with *her* favourite – bric-a-brac.

I've lost my touch, Jenny thought, as she physically held the women apart and prayed for deliverance. Working on the ward had been much easier. She'd been the boss and the nurses had been terrified of her: she barked, they ran to obey. Simple. But here she was dealing with *volunteers*; they couldn't be *told* what to do, she had to ask nicely, or, like today, beg, not that it was making any difference, they were ignoring her completely.

Oh, why had she ever taken the bloody job, she wondered, cursing her stupidity. She didn't *have* to work. Since mother had died, leaving her comfortably off, she'd been free to do as she pleased; but doing nothing, alone, had scared her.

'Rendering a service to the community,' that's what the advert had said. The way things were going, she was more likely to be rendering first aid or administering last rites. Thank God it was too early in the day for *that man* to be coming in, this debacle would have provided him with endless ammunition for his taunts. Come to think of it, she hadn't seen him for days, and suddenly, sickeningly, she knew why. Even Dot and Maisy, engaged in their shift changing ripostes, had been briefly united in their criticism of her.

'You shouldn't have said *that*,' Maisy had gasped.

'No,' Dot agreed, as they all stared at the trembling doorbell. 'Not to him. He's a *nice* man. A bit odd, but *nice*.'

Somewhat taken aback, Jenny had replied, 'Well, he shouldn't have provoked me.'

'He was only pulling your leg,' Maisy said, staring at Jenny as if she'd just grown another head.

'Yes, he's always doing that,' Dot agreed. 'Likes a bit of

fun does our Prof.'

'Fun!' Jenny spat.

'Some people just can't take a joke,' Maisy said.

'Mm,' Dot had grunted, 'which reminds me, Maisy; that window…' at which point their truce had ended, unlike Jenny's sense of guilt. She *was* too touchy, she knew that, but *that man* always knew which buttons to press.

He'd been haggling over the price of a teapot. Tears pricked her eyes. She'd lost a good customer because of a bloody teapot! But he was always arguing the toss and it annoyed her because she made a point of pricing things lower than the other charity shops in town.

'You're asking far too much,' he'd said, toying with its lid. 'I could buy one cheaper from the opposition up the road.'

'Then I suggest you do exactly that,' she'd retorted, making a grab for the teapot, which shot off the glass-topped counter and shattered at her feet.

'A somewhat exuberant selling technique, don't you think?' he'd enquired mildly, standing on tiptoe in order to inspect the debris.

'It's all your fault!' she'd snapped. 'By rights you should pay me for it.'

And he had, counting out the exact money in absolute silence before leaving the shop, closing the door behind him with exaggerated care.

No, he wouldn't be coming back to brighten her day…

'Stop it!' she screamed, all semblance of self-control finally deserting her, but the two women continued to struggle, battering at each other with handfuls of plastic roses.

ooooo

The acts of sabotage had been small-scale to begin with. The morning following 'Toy Story One', Maisy had laid out a teddy bears' picnic using some of Dot's bric-a-brac; that afternoon Dot had reciprocated by removing the bears and filling the space with a twenty-four-piece white and gold china tea service someone had generously donated. The deteriorating situation had not been helped by the fact that the tea service was purchased, at a very good price, early the following morning, before Maisy had a chance to change the window.

After that, the verbal exchanges at one-o'clock, as Maisy plodded out and Dot scuttled in, became minimal and glacial, until yesterday.

In preparation for Valentine's Day, Maisy had excelled herself; in fact she had been so busy that she'd lost track of time and was still hard at it when Dot arrived. The scene that followed had not been pretty, as Maisy tried to defend her fluffy, red, heart-shaped cushions and assorted containers of plastic red roses from Dot's onslaught.

Jenny had finally intervened with the suggestion that they dress half the window each. Maisy had stalked off to the back room laden down with superfluous hearts and flowers, and once she had left the shop, Dot gleefully dragged out a cardboard box containing a secret hoard that she'd obviously been collecting for months. Heart-shaped trinket boxes, rose-strewn china and ornamental plates inscribed with sickeningly sweet messages of love; she'd even managed to find a cherubic ceramic Cupid, poised, one-footed, on a briar-strangled pedestal. The contrasting styles of kitsch looked bizarre, and certainly stopped passers-by in their tracks. In fact, the shop had been busier than usual, and Dot, uncharacteristically, had

volunteered to refill the clothes rails whilst Jenny manned
the till all afternoon. It wasn't until Dot left, just after four
thirty, to bank the takings on her way home, that Jenny
discovered the results of her clandestine activities, and by
then it was far too late to single-handedly do anything
about it. Using the rush of customers as a smokescreen,
Dot had systematically stripped the window of all
remaining cushions and roses and set up, in their place,
a small folding table, covering it with empty champagne
bottles and glasses half-filled with a yellow liquid whose
origin Jenny didn't want to begin to think about. There
were even empty glasses strewn drunkenly around the legs
of the table.

When the shop emptied momentarily, Jenny had put
her head in her hands, telling herself that something
must be done before World War Three broke out, but her
attendances at management seminars had been years ago,
and they had never covered a situation like this. Praying
for inspiration, she'd picked up the phone.

The staff meeting did not go as planned. Jenny had wanted
a quick, peace making word with Maisy first, but she'd
arrived late and Dot had been early. They met outside the
shop window at ten o'clock. Jenny had not imagined it
possible for Maisy to break into a run, but run she did, and
within minutes was carrying out an armful of cushions
and roses from the back room whilst Dot tried to bodily
bar her way. To safeguard the public Jenny had locked the
shop door and flicked the sign to 'CLOSED'. When she
turned around the battle was in full swing. Hoping that
her tactics would work, Jenny had forced herself between

them, and waited…and waited…

Deliverance arrived, finally, and Jenny broke away to unlock the shop door.

'Mrs. Scriven? Mrs. Allsop?' the van driver called out.

Dot and Maisy, diverted from their tussle, turned as one towards the man, saying, 'Yes?'

'For you, ladies,' he said, grinning as he held out two bouquets of red roses.

Jenny stood back to avoid being trampled in the stampede as the women ran to collect their gifts.

'I wonder who they're from?' they said in unison as they opened the tiny envelopes.

'Mine says, "From a secret admirer",' Dot boasted.

Maisy giggled. 'Mine says, "Guess who loves you?" Look!'

Round-eyed, they examined one another's cards before turning to Jenny.

'None for you? What a pity!' Maisy smirked.

'She should try smiling instead of scaring customers off. Ow!'

Jenny bit on a 'serve-you-right' grin as Dot sucked her pricked thumb. Taking advantage of the momentary lull in hostilities, she said, 'Why don't you both take today off?' Raiding the till she added, 'Have a coffee together.' She whipped out another tenner, 'Have *lunch*; patch things up, mmm?' And get out of my sight, she thought.

Maisy rapidly palmed the proffered money but the pair had begun arguing again even before Jenny had opened the door for them.

'Bet yours came from Billy Wilkes,' Maisy teased Dot. 'He was soft on you in junior school.'

'Rubbish! Anyway, his wife keeps him on a tight leash.

Couldn't pick a dandelion without her permission. So who do you think yours are from, then?'

Maisy cast a wicked glance over her shoulder. 'Who knows? It could even be the Prof…'

Why such a petty taunt should hurt so much Jenny didn't know but she rushed back into the shop to escape further flack. If she'd been cleverer she could have avoided that wisecrack by ordering a bouquet for herself as well, because no one else would be, she thought. She began to tidy up the debris wearily, cramming roses into vases and replacing them in the window along with the cushions. Afterwards she surveyed the gaudy display with dismay, but was past caring enough to do anything about it. The causes of this mess could sort it out between themselves tomorrow.

Would their truce survive more than one day? Ahead lay a minefield of celebration days; Mothers' Day, Easter, Fathers' Day, and, perhaps most threateningly of all, Christmas. The very thought of that terrifyingly empty day sent Jenny dashing into the back room to make an extra strong mug of coffee. There were chocolate fingers and digestives in the tin, but they didn't appeal; somehow very little did. Not eating was one of the bad habits that she'd recently developed, along with drinking too much red wine.

Back at the counter Jenny flipped through an office supplies magazine, looking up every few moments towards the door, yet another of her bad habits.

This has *got* to stop, she told herself angrily, and began to attack the bookshelves with a duster, which reminded her that a boxful had been donated a few days ago and it still hadn't been sorted. He liked books; perhaps there would be something in there to interest him…

He won't be coming to look, she reminded herself, and swallowed. At least you won't have to listen to his sarcasm any more… And he's got a beard. Nasty things, beards. Unhygienic. You never knew what might be lurking in the undergrowth, and it would most probably tickle.

She tried to vacuum her wilful thoughts away, but all she could see, in her mind's eye, was an animated garden gnome darting around her shop, stopping only briefly to peer here, examine there.

'Like my hummingbird hawkmoth,' she whispered, and leant against the counter as she remembered over-long summer afternoons, drinking a solitary glass of wine or five, and watching, entranced, as the French visitor moved from honeysuckles to geraniums in high, arcing loops, never landing but hovering, sipping nectar from a bloom with its long proboscis, wings beating so rapidly that, when all else was still, she could hear a high-pitched hum. Its body seemed too squat and heavy for prolonged flight, its colouring a mediocre grey, but it was rendered magical by its stubby, fish-like tail; a drab mermaid, beautifully ugly, like him…and always alone…like her.

'Stop it, stop it!' she muttered, and bent to pick up the vacuum's hose that had slipped, unheeded, from her grasp. 'I don't care if I never see him again.'

She proved herself to be a liar two hours later, when, through the busy lunchtime throng, she spotted an unruly thatch of white hair, and the thumping in her chest told her how much she'd missed him.

'Rubbish!' she muttered, as she bent to pick up a customer's change that she'd just dropped on the floor. How could she possibly miss toothache?

She was totally distracted, however, trying to follow his erratic tour of the shop as he flitted from books to men's sweaters to nick-nacks, darting frequent sidelong glances at her through gaps in the milling customers. Finally, he selected an approved flight path and landed in front of her, grasping an ivory-handled letter opener.

'How much?'

'Pound.'

'Not worth it. Fifty pence.'

'Seventy five.'

'I've had flu. Have I missed anything special?'

'No, and it's still seventy five pence.'

He began rummaging clumsily in a pocket of his long cream raincoat with his right hand, holding his left arm stiffly by his side.

He's hurt himself, she thought, opening her mouth, then snapped it shut again. I am *not* going to ask, she told herself.

He poured some coins onto the counter. 'Is that enough?'

Jenny counted them. 'That's only sixty two pence!' Some of the customers laughed, and Jenny scooped the coins up hurriedly. 'All right,' she hissed. 'I'll let you get away with that trick this time, but don't try it on again!' forgetting in her anger to dodge the till drawer after she'd rung in the money, and it gave her a sharp thump in the ribs.

He pocketed the knife with bowed head. 'You're looking exceedingly ferocious today,' he finally said with a blue flick of his eyes, making it sound like a great compliment.

She gritted her teeth, but to no avail. '*You* look as if you've hurt yourself. Nothing trivial, I hope!'

He cocked his head to one side, as if sampling her

reaction, and she saw his beard shift in a covert smile.

And that's another thing, she thought furiously. You can't read a man's face when it's covered in wire wool. I can't tell what he's thinking. 'And I don't care,' she muttered to his retreating back as he darted off to examine the CDs.

As she served customers, Jenny recalled the few snippets of information, cautiously gleaned from Dot and Maisy about *that man*, so as not to arouse their curiosity, during her first few weeks in the job, but there was precious little to show for her efforts. He'd been a regular visitor to the shop for years; Maisy had heard he taught maths at the university and Dot said students sometimes called him the mad professor behind his back.

Mad? Yes! And I bet he's got an equally eccentric and brainy wife. Instead of making love they probably sit up in bed solving Sudoku Killers, doing the 'deadlies' against the clock to add a frisson of excitement.

Now where the hell had *that* thought sprung from, Jenny wondered. It's no concern of mine what he does. He means nothing to me. I don't even like him.

The number of customers in the shop gradually dwindled, and he made his erratic course back to the counter.

'Window's overdressed,' he pronounced, ringing the handbell marked 'Not for sale. Ring for attention'. Jenny felt like hitting him with it.

'All those roses. Too much sentiment.'

The fact that she actually agreed with him annoyed her so much that she felt compelled to argue the point. 'There's nothing wrong with roses and sentiment, in the right place,' she parried. 'It must be nice when somebody goes to the trouble of buying a bunch, to show someone that they care. I mean…' Her voice tailed off as she realised how pitiful she sounded, and she took her ire out on the tagging gun, almost fastening her finger to a blouse cuff in the process.

'How much for the Cupid?'

She stared at him in disbelief. 'That thing? It's hideous.'

'Oh, I think it has a certain *je ne sais quoi*.'

'Well, I don't know what it is, either, but it'll cost you a fiver.'

'I'll pick it up next week, and this time remember not to sell it.'

She ground her teeth, remembering her first day as manager. Maisy had set out to impress. The theme had been 'Bill and Ben', and the window's centrepiece a teetering pyramid of flowerpots. He had turned up and demanded, 'Bottom row, fourth from left looking in from the pavement.' He'd agreed to wait until the display was dismantled, but she'd forgotten to tell Maisy and Dot. The pot had been sold to someone else, and he was not going to allow her to forget it; ever.

Wrong-footed, she attacked nevertheless. 'The mind boggles as to where you put all this stuff. Your wife must get fed up, dusting it.'

'Haven't got a wife. She kicked me out years ago. Couldn't stand the mess. And you?'

'I haven't got a wife, either.' His beard twitched. 'Or a husband. He left me years ago because he couldn't stand my tidiness.' She thought of the regimented cushions that never needed plumping because no one ever relaxed against them, and shivered.

He picked up the bell again. 'Sounds very

unwelcoming.'

Stung, she lashed out, 'Well, it's better than a load of clutter. I'm surprised at you, being a mathematician. All those nice neat equations. I thought you would have had an orderly mind.'

'Physicist; and physics is chaotic. That's why I like it.'

'Well, I *hate* chaos!'

Over averted eyes, his shaggy brows began semaphoring in a language she could not comprehend, but she didn't need an interpreter to know that she had overstepped the mark. Twisting away to hide a sudden rush of tears she listened intently for his departure.

But there was only silence, and turning around cautiously she caught him doing an owl impersonation, rotating his head almost one hundred and eighty degrees in each direction, scanning the shop, and she realised with a start that it was empty.

Then he began to unbutton his coat with his right hand.

Oh, my God, he's going to flash! she thought, desperately trying to remember the shrivelling remarks she'd used when male patients demonstrated the progress of their recovery.

She slapped a hand over her mouth to stifle a hysterical giggle, which turned into a sob as he pulled out a package from beneath his coat. Bowing, he handed her a box of long-stemmed rosebuds, and for the first time met her gaze fully.

His eyes were electrifying, sparking with intelligence but also warm with a gentle humour that belied his machine gun repartée.

'My name is Henry,' he said quietly, 'and I think it's

time we met on neutral territory to solve this seemingly insoluble problem.'

Totally disarmed, Jenny could only gaze at him, speechless.

'Good. We're agreed on that, at least. Tomorrow. Twelve. Metropole Hotel. They do a good ploughman's. Don't be late.'

Before she could even attempt a reply, he turned and scurried towards the door.

'I'm never late!' she managed to shout, as he opened it, and he flapped her a quick wave as he passed the window.

Late? Jenny thought, hugging the roses to her breast. No way! She was going to arrive early and reconnoitre the joint; find a seat where subdued lighting would camouflage her wrinkles. Was there time to colour her hair? Oh, what was the point... He'd already seen her grey bits, many times; concealing them now would reveal too much.

She opened the box and caressed the blooms, knowing that the skirmishes were over. War had been declared, and the first battle would be tomorrow, at high noon.

The prospect made her smile.

Yellow Ribbons on a Pear Tree

Sian Melangell Dafydd

I have never met a killer. Not that I know. I saw a killer tree, once: the Strangling Fig Tree, not in the flesh but in a black and white newspaper cutting about foreign things. I thought of it selecting another tree, as indiscriminate as falling in love and, like a python, growing around its chosen one, intimately; large and muscular, killing by squeezing, by constricting, by suffocating.

The tree put strangling powers in my finger bones. I uprooted the acre of nettles covering the courtyard, pulling at the ragged edges of thick mature nettles. I didn't feel a single one of them rasp the skin of my palms. I pulled legs off spiders and saw them trying to run regardless. Maybe knowing we were at war made me violent. Maybe I wanted to contribute and Bruno wasn't going to clear my courtyard after being stupid enough to get himself imprisoned on a Welsh farm.

I think of this, reminding myself that Bruno has, in fact, returned. I have tangible proof: he is sweating in my bed. I wrap my arms around him and squeeze as tightly as I can but he slips in my arms like soap.

He sleeps. Sex has the opposite effect on me and I lie, stunned awake, looking through the crack between the closed shutters. Not that there's anything out there except a pear tree. A tender-edged thing like a low cloud. Harmless, unless I use the fruit to flavour grappa and then, combined, it's strong enough to scorch a body from the inside. Bruno, deflated, looks like he might need the fire of coffee rinsed with grappa but he'll open his eyes in about fifteen minutes. That's if he's the man I remember. He'll press tiny kisses on whatever part of my body is nearest his lips. In his sleep, he says, 'Gwylia'r danadl poethion,' and tickles the tiny hairs on my shoulder with his voice.

We have wrinkles on the bottom of our feet from the day we are born, like roots. Then, they grow around the tops of our feet and upwards. Bruno looks the same as always except for two things. He is now pale enough for me to think that Wales is under a rock, and the surface of his skin has become overgrown with wrinkles. He merges into the creases of my sheets. Against him, my tanned body looks like it's embracing a pile of linen.

He arrived home before dawn and had travelled all night. Women waited for men and, when the day started, the bus arrived. He stood in his deep green clothing and I could only see small patches of skin, but it was enough: fingers to cuffs, forehead to collar. His skin had gone to seed. He smelt of soil as if he'd been planted in it.

He said 'bella,' and I thanked him. He didn't say what or who was 'bella,' and I didn't comment on how he looked. We walked and, as if nothing had changed, we took our old shortcut home by the low waters of the Piave and through Basso's sweetcorn field, walking side by side and apologising silently with a nod every time we brushed shoulders. When he spoke again, I was pleased to hear his voice. It came out foreign.

'Gwylia'r danadl poethion.'

'What?'

'Gwylia'r danadl poethion,' he said as if I was deaf or stupid or both. I turned around to see his mouth and the place where the strange words came from as I walked straight into the daggered long grass full of nettles and yelped.

He stood back. His eyes were clear as cream but, in them, I could almost see the cogs of his mind turning; thoughts of Italy tipping into those eyes, slowly curdling his view. He pleated his eyebrows and asked, 'Did that come out in the wrong language?'

'Yes!' I pointed to my leg, skin not yet rising into red bubbles, both of us knowing it would.

'I'm tired.'

I scratched furiously. 'What language was it?'

'Welsh. I meant, "watch the nettles".'

'Too late.'

'Are you hurt?'

'Yes.'

He yanked my hand away from my leg to stop me from scratching. He nodded and went on his way through the nettles, holding them aside with a deliberate, calm and calloused hand as if not to startle the green enemy. I followed, walking through each section he had cleared. I didn't tell him that I hadn't used that path for years until we arrived in the kitchen and my legs were covered in boiling skin.

I put a saucepan of salted water on the gas, 'Pastasciutta?'

'Please. My legs are hollow.'

I laid the table: plates for tripe under bowls for pastasciutta, his mother's napkins and best tumblers, our wedding cutlery and crusty white rolls. I drank a glass of prosecco like water before pouring his.

'What did they feed you there?'

'Not spaghetti.'

He didn't mark his chin with tomato stripes by sucking his spaghetti. Someone has taught him to be tidy.

We lunched early, cut the day short, came to bed before bedtime and now all I want is for him to wake up. The day and our bodies are still heating. We have time, and he has layers of skin on him that I know nothing about.

He needs sun in him, pulp and colour, tomato and black wine. I think he's been painted all over in egg white. Sweat dries. His new skin might harden in this position, sleeping solid. I hear less beat to his breathing. He doesn't twitch or stir nor show any sign of rousing.

A box was waiting for us when we arrived back at the house. He said that it was sent by post the day after he left Bachwared. Bless him; he doesn't expect me to be able to pronounce that. The box almost beat him here.

'Boxes are easier to deliver than men,' he said, 'boxes don't have to sign papers.' He has done nothing all day except sit in the shade and eat Welsh cake from his box. Delivered with the cake were photographs of a grey house and a letter full of exclamation marks. He didn't show them to me. I just looked over his shoulder. He gave me a piece of the cake to eat and I chewed it for so long I got bored, so I spat it out at the other end of the vine grove.

'There's a bowl of fresh fruit in the kitchen. Eat from that,' I told him over and over until he replied, 'What a pity we have nothing to send them back but fruit. It would arrive rotten, wouldn't it?'

Grappa: that's one way of preserving fruit but I won't remind him, or he'll want to send some to the enemy.

'What were they like to you, the Welsh?' If he had killed, I wondered, was it one of them, before he lived among them.

'I don't know,' he said. As a second thought, he said, 'We kept watch for fox together at night. Fox kill sheep. We drank whisky to keep awake.'

'Whisky?'

'Good drink, like rusty grappa.'

'I'll make some.'

'You can't make whisky.'

'But I can make grappa.'

So that's the plan. It will be clear and sharp as flame with the delicacy of pear aromas to entice him to drink. It will burn all other tastes from his gums and leave fruit sugar around his teeth for me to kiss out. His arrival is perfect timing for my grappa: the pears are all firm and smaller than the mouths of bottles.

I collected all the old wine bottles and slipped one over every fruit on the tree. Some of the bigger pears had to be brushed with olive oil to lubricate them into the glass, but I've squeezed a bottle on every pear and secured them to the tree by ribbon I ripped out of an old yellow blouse. Branches heave, heavy.

When the pears are fully grown and trapped inside their bottles I'll snip them off at the stalk and let them rattle in their bottles, tasty little messages, and let the branches whip up again. I'll douse the pears in grappa.

Let the tastes come together. Let the alcohol energy strike Bruno at the back of his throat and bring him home.

But I hear the delicate crash of breaking glass, a crunch like garlic skin. I imagine un-bruised fruit and a shattered bottle where the nettles used to be. Bruno curls up into a foetal position and turns away; his two soiled, still brown soles face me. The bedsheets are full of his cake spices. Their smells snake out of him in sweat, spit and semen and strangle me like constricting branches at my throat.

Holm Oak

Naomi Bagel

The first time the gypsies called to our front door was the Halloween that I celebrated my tenth birthday. Few visitors called to our house, not surprisingly, since it was only in the spring of that year that we had moved there and we had no contacts in the area. Sussex was where I had lived all my life, before we relocated to the New Forest to a huge isolated house. However, it satisfied Mothers' craving for grandeur.

The air was rich with the scent of earth and dying summer leaves that morning when I watched the group walking up our drive. They were led by a jaunty grey-haired man wearing a navy blue suit that displayed a canary yellow jumper underneath his jacket. An emerald green scarf was folded round his neck and tied together in the front. I observed that the scarf was secured by a gold tie-pin fashioned in a horseshoe shape.

Beside him walked a diminutive woman whose movements possessed the bearing of royalty. Her thick grey hair was braided into plaits jauntily decorated with poppy red ribbons. Striding purposefully, this woman displayed all the grace of good posture that I completely failed to manifest, despite both deportment lessons and being regularly beaten for my lack of coordination.

I marvelled at her tiny feet, encased in the sort of sturdy leather boots that boys wear. These boots were well polished and were set off by a pair of gaily striped woollen socks. She wore a thick skirt in the same shade of red as her ribbons with rows of ric-rac braid and bright tapes stitched in rows around the hem. The skirt ended near the place where her socks began. A flash of bronzed leg showed as the skirt swung forward. Her tweed riding jacket fitted her snugly and somehow the whole image she presented conjured up, for me, the gypsy queen from the old legends, one who was born of the earth, mortal for the period of her reign, her destiny to return to the earth spirits again. This fascinating couple was followed by a pair of young men, who I hardly noticed in any detail as my eyes were full of the sight of her.

My Mother was tall with auburn hair and stood five foot eight inches in her stockings before she put on the high-heeled shoes that she greatly favoured. When she opened the front door, I was spellbound by the disparity in their height and character.

The woman spoke to my mother, introducing the whole group by stating in a gentle voice carrying undertones of a musical lilt, 'We're the Coopers.' Her quiet demeanour did not disguise the power and strength that had made a profound impression on me. I was ten years old, an avid reader, oozing with a quest for knowledge and unbounded enthusiasm for encountering some of the colourful characters that I had met in books.

I gave Mother a swift sideways glance for the purpose of evaluating her reaction. I knew that I was waiting for her to make a cuttingly acerbic pronouncement. I cringed in anticipation of her words, feeling the breakfast that I had eaten earlier turning into a ball of concrete in my stomach. I didn't want to hear her disapproval because I had fallen in love with Mrs Cooper and all that she represented to me.

Before Mother could say anything the woman spoke again, her unfathomable brown eyes looking deep into Mother's wide green ones.

'You're strange to this house.' It wasn't a question, it was a statement, 'And you are strange to the ways of the forest.'

Mother stood in silence while my gypsy queen asked to be granted permission to cut holly ivy and other leaves from the bottom of our garden as it was the time of year when they made wreaths to sell. Apparently the tradition had been long established and this entitlement had passed through generations of Coopers, who called when the days shortened to cut greenery.

'Well, my lovely,' she began, 'we usually cut in the bottom garden, in the wild by the forest fence, and prune out the pretty ivy on the kitchen garden wall. Cutting the growth back and letting us bear away the trim outs keeps your green in good heart as well as bringing you the fortune of a gypsy's blessing.'

'Go and get on with it then,' answered Mother, 'and take the girl with you, she will show you the gate to the forest. You can use that entrance instead of trooping up the drive.'

The front door shut resolutely.

'We don't need you to show us around.' Mrs Cooper looked at me, and I became conscious of being exceedingly grubby, my jumper covered with sawdust from cutting up logs for the winter fire. I understood that she was speaking kindly and wasn't dismissing me.

'This earth around here and myself knows each other

like the back of my hand. My parents brought me here when I was a little chavvy in wraps. I know what grows hereabouts. Soon you will too.'

She pointed to a compact tree that grew to the left of the house. I had admired the textured darkness of its trunk and was surprised when the autumn came, to discover that it was an evergreen.

'That be a Holm oak,' she declared proudly, 'I've watched it grow over the years. One of our ancestors brought it back from his travels and planted it here. Four hundred years that tree has known my family.'

Mother was certainly not an appreciator of a garden, nor ever had been. She also had very little desire to sit outdoors or to rummage around in the countryside. Having given the Coopers the permission they had requested Mother declared there was no need to speak to them ever again.

We had five acres of land including a paddock, a walled kitchen garden, a vast lawn with shrubbery and a considerable amount of woodland separated from the New Forest by a post and wire fence with a gate. Mother stated that she really didn't give a damn if they wanted to cut holly or 'goodness knows what,' from the bushes, there was plenty enough stuff growing around the place.

I mentioned that having gypsies around for the greenery would bring good luck to the house, and she got very angry, and beat me with the riding crop that she kept for that purpose. When I looked into her eyes I knew that she was afraid of what might happen if she crossed the gypsies.

Royston, the gardener, cycled up from the village

three days a week to keep the garden in order. He was familiar with the grounds, having worked for the previous owners and recommended that Mother should rent out the paddock for grazing. Of course he was acquainted with the very person who would be interested, so a fat pair of ponies munched serenely away in the pasture all summer.

The Coopers came and went intermittently over the next few weeks, they had taken to quietly cutting and trimming what they needed. Missus showed me to cut the greenery without damaging next year's crop, and to lay it out in baskets doing no harm to this year's bounty. I asked few questions, but I listened.

On the front doorstep one morning I discovered a beautiful wreath that had been fashioned from glossy holly, rich with red berries and intertwined with two-toned ivy. The whole thing was bejewelled with patches of pale green mosses. I understood that the time had come when the Coopers moved on, their work finished. Entranced with the beautiful gift I carried it carefully to Mother, who immediately disliked it, instructing me to dispose of 'that damn thing,' because it was too funereal.

I took it away and hung it from a six inch nail on a beam in the old stable, a place that Mother would never visit. She had declared it was not only unsafe with falling plaster, but filthy with spiders as well. Inevitably, her antipathy to the stable made it a safe place for me. I kept a few books there and they had not been eaten by rats. I stood on a rusty oil drum to hang the wreath up. When I stood to admire it I noticed a few fruits of the Holm oak had been worked in as well. To me it was a queen's crown, a jewelled circlet, a thing of great loveliness.

I grew up in that big house in the forest and each Halloween the passing years were marked by the Coopers. Always Mr and Missus, at times the boys, sometimes women and children, arrived. When I was old enough, in an effort to help our family fortunes, I set up a chicken farm on the paddock. It was a more profitable use of the land than grazing a pair of sluttish ponies just to keep the grass down.

I started the business originally with Erik, a friend of Mother's, an alcoholic who had once served in the Fleet Air Arm. He told me he had seen things that turned him towards drink to block the images out of his head. That seemed fair enough, until he drank himself into such an appalling state that his mind and his body was ablaze with horrific images, and he had to be hospitalised.

Mother would have no more to do with him, so I carried on with the chicken farm by myself, employing a few village boys. By now there were 25,000 chickens being reared for the table. Five thousand in each large chicken house; buy them in at day old, rear them to Sunday dinner size on deep litter and try to keep as many as possible alive. Sometimes something dreadful would happen; a flooding water trough and many birds would die of a chill; a thunderstorm, and they would pile into one corner; a power cut or illness. I wouldn't want to do that job again, but at the time it seemed all right.

I appreciated watching the change in the seasons; the new green of spring with wood anemones, summers' blowsy blossoms and heady perfumes. When leaves began to change their colours the Coopers would enter noiselessly through the forest gate, and go about their business of garnering the greenery. They became part of the rhythm of life and somehow, without words, I knew when they were around and we never failed to meet up.

Over the years I had built up quite a little collection of Christmas wreaths, hung up on nails that I hammered into the beams of the stable. A draught blew over the top of the door drying every leaf, turning moss into feathered fronds. Each was individual in its artistry; all were delicately beautiful, each with pieces from the Holm oak woven someplace in the wreath.

The winter when the rhododendrons bloomed on Christmas Eve was followed by snow that fell in January covering my world in a white veil, creating a strikingly handsome landscape. It made many jobs on the farm more difficult with everything icy and frozen. The paths were iced, the boys appeared intermittently for work and I battled to keep the water drinkers flowing and worried about the electricity failing.

Sometimes a thaw would set in and the roof snow on the chicken houses would melt, dripping noisily over the day until, mid-afternoon, the ambient temperature would drop and icicles re-formed. Frozen stalagmites and stalactites developed longer and taller as snow fell upon snow that had lain on the ground for nearly a month. I become conscious that my life and my world had become constrained within the boundaries of Mother's large house and the five acres of garden within which it was situated.

When at last the snow finally began to melt I made myself the time to take a walk through the grounds. I followed the boundary fence, looking for the brave snowdrops that were already showing their heads through the melting slush. I continued walking, and suddenly the ground gave way beneath me, I lost my footing and was sitting on my bottom on the soft leaf mould. I was surprised, and thought I had stumbled over a tree root, before noticing I had fallen into an indentation in the ground, about nine inches deep, two feet wide and five feet long that had not been there before.

I knew what it was before I noticed the tiny tufts of Holm oak, holly and ivy that were scattered around. Beyond any shadow of doubt I knew that I was sitting on Mrs Cooper's grave, Missus buried here to rest in peace. It felt like a sacred trust to honour this secret, so I fetched a shovel for the purpose of back filling the soil where it had sunk down. That seemed a practical thing to do.

I levelled off the earth, scattering twigs and dead leaves over. It didn't seem in any way peculiar that these Romany travellers who lived by their own laws should have chosen this quiet spot in the woods to bury their queen, whose family had more connection and roots with the place than Mother and I. It was a privilege that she had been laid to rest here.

Maybe some folk would think my intuition was the product of an overheated imagination sparked by the narrow life that I lived on those five acres. I know it wasn't, for when the spring came, small flower garlands appeared, they were hung on the trees near the grave with jaunty little red ribbons like those on Missus's plaits decorating them.

When the Coopers arrived after Halloween, I did not expect to see Missus but I saw a flash of her skirt and bright socks through the bushes, before I was close enough to see it was her daughter Rosy, with her thick hair plaited and tied with green ribbons. Mr Cooper, whose style of dress had changed very little over the years, held out his hand to me. I took it and he said, 'We normally fires up the wagon that they lived in, with them inside when they die. It's tidy. It's always been done that way, but my girl didn't want that. She's from mixed blood, and she always said that she wanted to rest here.'

Letting go of his strong brown hand, all I could say was, 'Thank you, for trusting me with her.'

I knew as the seasons turned the Coopers would come and go, although Missus was no longer with them her vibrancy lived and danced in the hearts and minds of the many who loved her, and this was evident in the small floral tributes that I would find near the forest fence.

Time did not sweeten Mother, nor did the glory of a spring morning ever fire her spirit; a sunset never warmed her soul. I wouldn't choose her final resting place with anything like the care or love the Coopers had for the Missus. Mother's grandchildren never knew her, she died before they had a chance to soften her with their unconditional love.

Secrets of the Potting Shed

Ruth Joseph

I've always been inspired by potting sheds ever since my Bampi first carried me on his broad-shouldered back, into his secret place of damp smells, sacks of well rotted manure, and the first flanks of seedlings pushing twin-paired leaves out of the dark alongside their soldiered labels. He'd lower me gently onto a Jaffa packing case, topped with one of Gran's old cushions, which served as a spare seat, while he took the old rocker, wink at me and say: 'Cup of tea, lovee? But don't tell Gran, eh? I'll be shot if I give you the proper stuff instead of that old milky drink she gives you.'

Then he'd light up an old Primus stove balanced on a piece of tarry black slate, readjusting the paraffin in the small metal container; I'd wrinkle my nose at the smell. And after a fight with some damp matches, he'd eventually coax a flame, tease water out of a squeaky brass tap, pouring it into the kettle, its outside charred with years of use. An old dusty tea caddy would come off the shelf next to ancient packets of powdered bonemeal, whatever that was, and a vital plastic tub of hormone rooting powder. (And teatime, when I dipped my soldiers into my boiled egg, I overheard my mother whispering on the phone that Aunty Vi had to take HRT for her flushes and I knew she must have gone to Bampi's potting shed and used that pot, because we all knew that he could make everyone better with his magic.) He'd warm a Brown Betty teapot with a little of the heated water, swishing it round with a grand flourish, discarding that liquid outside the shed, then he'd add the loose tea leaves and pour on fresh boiling water, telling me all the time that, 'You can't get a decent cup unless the water's really hot and you use proper loose tea – none of that dust rubbish they put into those silly poncey bags. The world's gone convenience mad, kid.' And I'd nod in agreement, resting a chubby face on dimpled hands. He'd hand me a plastic mug full of the liquid – dark and rich and thick, like the linseed oil in the jam jar on another shelf near the tea caddy, adding milk from a screw top bottle out of his pocket. From the back of the shelf next to the plastic labels he'd made out of washing-up liquid bottles, he'd produce a rusted Huntley and Palmer's biscuit tin full of custard creams, garibaldi biscuits and fig rolls.

I loved the biscuits but I wasn't sure about the brew, although I never said and now I insist on drinking it the same way.

After our snack, we'd go out past the greenhouse full of growing produce, to the vegetable patch, and cut a lettuce, and lengths of rhubarb thick like giant's walking sticks, then pull some radishes or pluck ripe berries that Gran would turn into a crumble or pie, mixed with some tart Bramleys, and serve alongside a jug of rich creamy custard to go with our tea.

Then Bampi and Gran passed away and someone else took over Bampi's potting shed. I took up with Eric – a spotty, gangling lad in the same year in school. He bore a strong resemblance to Mick Jagger and later, on dark lonely nights, when I asked myself why, I could only assume that must have been the initial reason for the attraction. We drifted together. Call it a geographical attachment – he lived up the road, and our mothers were friendly. As children we'd shared trips to Porthcawl, bags of chips and shivered under a towel together. Now, after a few trips to the pictures, a couple of meals and some experimental fumbles in the front parlour, people began asking, my mother included. Finally we became engaged with the date set.

Our marriage took place on a wet November lunch time, and a few of his family and ours sat down to a meal of greasy chicken and half-defrosted mandarin cheesecake washed down with warm Cava in a grubby room above the Lazy Fox. My dress came from Barnardos and there never was a ring: his excuse was that we were saving for a place of our own, so I wore Gran's old gold band and treasured its worn smoothness over my finger.

From the outset there was never that passion between us that I saw in others. I'd watch them in the pictures, sat next to Eric, gazing with wonder at the film stars acting out their torrid scenes and, around us, others loving in the dark. While with my new husband, it was a beery three minute consideration on a Saturday night, after last orders. And then even that disappeared from our lives. We seemed to be moving in separate circles – Eric home at odd hours, his mind in other places, his head stuck behind the sheets of the daily rag, as he barked out his needs like a demented hound. He'd wait for his meal to be served on the kitchen table, pour over copious amounts of ketchup, substitute my laid knife and fork for a spoon, then take it to the couch in the sitting room, spooning loads into his fleshy, cavernous mouth. He'd belch loudly a few times, pat his growing belly, then leave the plate on the floor for the dog to finish, bits of gravy flicking up onto the upholstery. After his meal, Eric'd switch up the volume of the old black and white to insufferable, always on the football, turn his body to the wall and fall asleep snoring loudly. I abandoned the idea of being in the same room as him as the mindless chanting and drumming on the television, coupled with his snoring, shook the place with a hellish vibrato.

So, when I'd completed the chores, I spent my spare time listening to a different world on the radio, planting orange and lemon pips on the kitchen windowsill and watching the small glossy leaves appearing. As the tiny saplings grew, I used to imagine I could see them as mature trees bearing fruit sitting in the hot Mediterranean sun in Southern Italy, Spain or Morocco. I'd look at the side of the delivery boxes in the supermarket and read the place of origin and let my imagination do the rest. I asked Eric for a garden but he liked our patch of concrete outside the back door: 'maintenance free', and even complained when I placed a few pots with daffs there in the spring, replacing them with geraniums in the summer, that they were a 'sheer waste of money', and in his way when he parked the car. And once he 'accidentally' reversed the car into a plastic pot of tulips, mashing them with his tyres so that they crushed into a bleed of brown compost stained with pink and red.

There were no children in the marriage and, as we became older, Eric became a bitter man complaining at my every move and carping on about the cost of everything; even cutting back on the housekeeping. As he moaned, I mourned our empty relationship. For a long time I'd wanted more. I wanted to share the beauty of a spider's web when the early dew had decorated it with tiny rainbow drops. I wanted to walk in a garden that I had helped to grow and admire the purple and indigo spires of delphiniums mingled with pink and purple-throated foxgloves and hollyhocks: chase laughing through copper beech trees in the autumn and kick through their crisp russet leaves. I wanted to dance cheek to cheek with a lover who held me tight in his arms and whispered words of endearment in my ear. I wanted to sit at opposite ends of a bath with rose petals floating on the surface of the water and, later, make love in the hot, sweet quietness of an afternoon with the float of a curtain blowing in the breeze, moaning with pleasure in a lover's arms. But I would have settled for friendship in the marriage or just to be noticed.

I could never understand the reason for Eric's exhaustion. After all, he sat at a desk in the Post Office. And why so tardy? Often ten pm and later… He always maintained that he was hoping for promotion and had to work long into the evening to prove his worth. But, on Thursday the 2nd of March, all was revealed. I was going through the pockets of his trousers before washing them and found a serrated cardboard section from the front of a box of tissues. On it in an unfamiliar hand were the words, 'sausages, passata, nice cauli, four large onions, packet of loo rolls and porridge oats'. A shopping list in a stranger's writing. I sat down bewildered; my hands clammy and a feeling of nausea overwhelming my body. As I stared at this piece of foreign cardboard in my hands, I suddenly realised the reason for the exhaustion. Someone else was enjoying my Eric. I wasn't angry, well not straight away, more flummoxed that he would want another or that anyone would find him sexually attractive. But later the resentment increased. I remembered his cruelty to my tulips – his manacle-hold on my life. From that moment I resolved to change my circumstances forever.

Days before I'd seen an advert in a local paper, 'Potting shed available to keen gardener in exchange for share of produce.' Up until now I'd hesitated. I knew Eric would resent my involvement in another place even if he wasn't home. The next day, as soon as Eric left, I telephoned. A pleasant man's voice answered.

'Oh, yes. Come and have a look. See if you could manage to change it; well, it's such a shame. Mother would be so upset.'

Just a bus ride away and a different world… as I walked down the street I could hear the faint sound of a lawnmower cutting the first moss-scented rush of grass. Here the rows of houses had room to breathe, with green borders and trimmed hedges surrounding flower beds burgeoning with the first spring bulbs. A few of the crocuses were still in flower but it was the hyacinths and the daffodils that were boasting their gaudy presence, and a few of the houses had their own magnolia tree; still in blossom, their pink and creamy-white candelabra emitted the very faintest perfume.

I knocked on the door of number 30, Woolacombe Drive. A man, maybe in his late forties, blinked through polished lenses, smiled and outstretched his arm.

'Hi. Mrs Dawkins? Good to see you. I'm Gilbert Smedley – second violin – that's the problem, a musician you see, not a gardener. Please come in.'

I followed Gilbert through a stained glass porch filled with dying plants that craved my attention, into a large open-plan room with a grand piano curved into a bay on the far side and a window seat plumped full of chintz cushions in soft pinks and browns in the other bay. Between this symmetry were French windows. Gilbert opened both doors wide and more sun poured in with the sound of animated bird song and a gentle wind through the surrounding trees. Outside in the garden, flanking one creosoted fence, sat a potting shed together with a small but perfect greenhouse.

'Yes, that's them – the potting shed and the greenhouse. Follow me. I'm sure you know far more about this gardening lark than I do. And poor Mum was so proud of her plants.'

He opened the door to the potting shed and instantly there was that damp, musty perfect scent. I gasped.

'Oh I know it's in a terrible mess…but do you think?'

'I'd love to try…'

In my mind I was recreating Bampi's rows of seedlings, and potting them off into bigger pots and sitting them in the greenhouse. There I'd planted tall branches of tomatoes with their trusses of herby yellow flowers and here I was picking off the side shoots to encourage a stronger growth. I could see cucumber and sweet pea seedlings *cwtched* in a propagator and maybe a melon plant in the greenhouse and I'd just read about *Physalis* grown from seed and wanted the challenge.

Gilbert shrugged his shoulders. 'I'm afraid this is the greenhouse – it used to be my mother's pride and joy.' In the corner, was a vine, barely alive, punctuated with a few yellowing leaves, surrounded by a host of weeds. I knelt before the vine and automatically began picking off the dead leaves.

'Where's the tap? It's desperate for a drink. I'll soon get it looking a bit healthier…if that's all right.'

'Please carry on. I'd be delighted.'

Two years have passed and I can hear Gilbert practising Greig, following it with a Bruch piece he has to perfect for Thursday's concert. I hum, picking out the strains of the music that have become part of my life. I'm in the potting shed with a plastic mug of dark mahogany tea sitting at my side as I prick out my tiny basil and fennel seedlings from the propagator into larger pots. When I've finished and scrubbed the vestiges of the rich compost off my fingers, I'll return to the house. I've planned a leek and potato soup for supper, made out of my own stored leeks and potatoes from last year's harvest. There's a fresh granary loaf proving on top of the oven and a few raspberries I managed to keep and freeze from the summer's canes, in one of Gran's dishes, to follow. That is when Gilbert has finished practising and we have shared a bath.

The Bottle Garden

Joy Tucker

Walk along the seafront at Swansea. Look up at layer upon layer of houses clinging to the hill and you can see where our garden used to be. It had to be a sunny day to see it properly then. Not far past the old Slip Bridge (it has gone now, too), there was a place where my sister and I would turn our heads and look up to see the sparkle of what our father called his 'diamond'. And to him it really was his most precious possession. My sister Ruby and myself (I'm Pearl) were his other special possessions. And when I once asked my mother, a plain-named Jane, why these particular names had been chosen, she said, 'Your father's choice of course.'

I mentioned this to Ruby a couple of days after our father's funeral.

'It could have been worse,' she said. 'It's a wonder we're not Hyacinth and Chrysanthemum.'

'Don't be so hard on him,' I said.

'Look who's talking!' was her reply.

We had gone for a walk along the foreshore, and sure enough, when we came to the spot we both remembered, our heads turned automatically to look up to the hill. And the diamond was still sparkling in the September sun, outshining, as it always had done, the other gardens around it. I should explain…

First of all it wasn't diamond-shaped – just a small

rectangle in a line of other rectangles. What made it different was that there were no trees, no bushes, no grass. Simply flowers. Lines of flowers, regiments of flowers. From the first daffodils, through tulips, hyacinths, delphiniums, hollyhocks, gladioli, chrysanthemums and a variety of roses, each flower stood alone and apart, each stem encased for its lifetime in a cylinder of glass, made from old bottles and jars. There were no weeds in this bottle garden; no wild flower seeds, wafted in on the soft west wind, were allowed to stay. There was no way for snails or slugs to eat holes in the well guarded blooms, no comfort zone for wandering cats; not a bench to sit on for gazing out over the sea at the blue hills of Devon, nowhere to play, nowhere to dig a tunnel. There was only a glass army of collected bottles filled with protected flowers that were never picked.

'Do you think Mam will want to do something with the garden?' I asked. 'As a hobby, I mean. She could do with an interest. You know, when I come to think of it, has she ever had an interest – apart from Dad and us that is?'

'We'd better get home,' Ruby said. 'We shouldn't have left Mam on her own so soon. I'm going to persuade her to come back with me for a break.'

'She won't go. I've already asked her to come back with me, and she said no.'

We found ourselves hurrying home, breathless from rushing up the hill – laughing when we reached the top, remembering the times we had hurried in the past, and then looking guiltily at each other as we realised there was not the same need to hurry. There was no one now to pull us in the door, to set us around with restrictions, to protect us, to keep us safe. *No, you can't go. Mustn't be late. Not safe at night. Where have you been? Who were you with?* No wonder we had both left home as soon as we could, and both after a blazing row with our father. Ruby went first, vowing never to come back; but of course she did. And I followed a little more quietly. It was a delicious escape – to a mad desire for freedom, followed by waves of unexpected homesickness and then a settling down to managing reality, making lives for ourselves. After that we were never home for any length of time. A snatched day here and there, a Christmas, an anniversary, occasions allowing little time to talk.

It was a difficult time, around the funeral, for talking. There was the shock and the sadness to deal with – the attempts to cope with unexpected lumps in the throat, eyes that wouldn't stay dry, the embarrassment of watching other people having the same problems. But on the night before our walk, when the distant relatives had gone, and all the neighbours had paid their respectful visits, Ruby produced a bottle of wine, and the three of us, the mourning women, sat down together and really talked. Well, Ruby and I talked, and talked, and I think our mother listened. All she said about our father was, 'He looked after us well.' She had a faraway look in her eyes as she spoke. And quite suddenly, I had this vision of the three of us – our pretty flower heads protruding from a row of bottles, separate, apart, untouching, untouchable. And I have never felt so alone in my life.

The walk by the sea had been my idea. Mam had some business to see to, and I wanted some fresh air and a chance to tell Ruby how strangely I had felt. She listened, and for a moment her face showed a quickly hidden flicker of recognition. 'It must have been the wine,' she said. 'We've all got to get back to normal. Life has to go on.'

Mam was still out when we reached home.

'I hope she's all right.' Ruby sounded worried, then irritated. 'Pearl, do you have a key?'

'You're joking! Dad never thought I was old enough to have a key!' We stood in the street, where only sometimes had we been allowed out to play, and felt awkward. 'We'd better wait in the garden,' I suggested.

'What garden?' Ruby's tone was moving from irritation to sarcasm. I had forgotten what an angry older sister she could be as she stomped around to the back of the house.

In the garden it was chrysanthemum time. Rows of shaggy bronze and yellow heads stood in haughty glass-encased lines. The sun was going down, trailing pink clouds behind Mumbles Head. 'Do you remember the time we all went to Cefn Bryn for the Summer Solstice – and how Dad was so mad when Mam told him she had given permission?'

'How could I forget?'

'Do you remember the way he would be waiting outside every party or Club we ever went to?'

'It was so embarrassing! But Ruby, do you ever wish you hadn't gone away?'

'No – why are you asking that?'

'All this reminiscing, I suppose – time passing – losing Dad, Mam on her own. I don't know. Maybe I've grown up.'

'Look,' said Ruby, very much the big sister, 'we felt we were being smothered, mollycoddled, overprotected...'

'Safe?' I suggested.

A sudden swirl of starlings passed over our heads in a

black, shrill cloud. 'I wish Mam would come home,' said Ruby. 'It'll be dark soon.' The fading light was taking the sparkle from the garden.

'I used to watch Dad make his plant bottles,' I told her. 'He tied string soaked in paraffin around the top and bottom of each bottle, set fire to the string, tapped the bottle with a hammer, and hey presto!'

'Bet you weren't allowed to do it!'

'No, but I could. I'll show you if you like.'

'I thought you said you'd grown up.' Ruby was brightening. 'Go on, then. Show me!'

We sounded like children again, but undaunted I opened the lean-to in the corner of the garden, bent down to take the hammer from a shelf, and immediately bumped my head against our mother's new shoes. I knew they were her new shoes, because she'd needed black shoes for the funeral and I had gone shopping for them with her just a week before. I looked above the shoes and, unbelievably, saw our mother hanging there – alone and so lonely in the bottle garden – quite unprotected and quite dead. And all I could hear then was Ruby screaming.

I stayed on at home after all the fuss was over, after Ruby had gone and there were no more questions to ask each other. *Had she loved him too much? Had she loved him at all? Was it his fault? Or ours? Would we ever know? Why? Why, Mam, why?* And when the house had been sold and it was time for me to leave, I ventured once more into the lean-to. I found the hammer, and, swinging it strongly and systematically, I walked up and down my father's diamond of a garden, crashing it against each and every bottle and jar. Shards of glass flew around and I almost wished that their jagged edges would fly at me, ripping my skin. Somehow it would have seemed fitting for some of my blood to be spilt in that careful, blighted place. Neighbours came out to see what the noise was and to ask if I was all right. I walked away then, my feet crunching on a gravel of glass, leaving the sad, battered flowers to mourn their brief freedom.

Falling Meadow

Alexandra Claire

When everywhere else was touched by the cool sea breeze, Falling Meadow was always warm, damp and sweet. When a cloud passed in front of the sun, it subdued rather than stole the warmth.

It had been named Falling Meadow since our grandfather, who had thought the land too steep even for potatoes, had let it go to meadow while he decided its best use. Since then, two generations of us Davies children had tumbled, rolled and fallen down its steep, soft gradient. In early summer, the girls had sat immersed in the rippling waves of grass, making daisy chains, blowing at dandelion clocks or determining the leanings of a beau by the age-old method of picking petals from wild flowers. The boys had fought wars, as boys do, commanders with imaginary infantry making a jungle of the high summer grass.

When the hay was to be made, we children would hang our heads and drag our feet to the meadow, cajoled into helping the hands to make quick work of it, knowing that we would now have to search for new homes to house our secrets and nurse our imaginations. We vented our anger with each swing of a billhook and slice of the scythe so that by the time the grass was laid to dry, we were already thinking of woodland dens and coppice hideaways.

ooooo

My brothers had gone away to war and my sister to drive ambulances in London, but I remained at home. Falling Meadow was the place where I could still find them. It ran with the echoes and shadows of us all. I would pass through it on my Tuesday walk to the village and I swear I could breathe them all in. I stopped to sit just the once; closed my eyes, let the sun set a kaleidoscope of shapes inside my eyelids, and I inhaled the essence of my siblings; Jack, Donald and Pixie. I laughed out loud and rolled down the slope spinning and spinning until my eyes opened and tears fell. I wanted Pixie. I missed them all, but I had to fight hard every day not to shatter into pieces without Pixie. A year apart in age, until the war we'd not been apart for as much as a day. I walked on to the village, picking grass shrapnel from my skirt and sweater, angry at myself for those tears. I couldn't afford to indulge in nostalgia, none of us could; my mother, father and grandfather, we just carried on, swallowing our fear, tightening our throats and filling hours of doubt with silence. Sometimes, my throat would be sore with unexpressed sorrow. I wanted to scream but was more afraid that my secret indulgence would be heard.

There is a relentless rhythm to farm life. My own temperament suited the structure that the land imposed. I had always run happily in the maze of this routine, growing more attached to the familiarity of the twists and turns with the passing of each year. Pixie was different. As we got older she talked of unseen places, but finding that I did not share her longing to leave she began to brood alone, imprisoned by the certainty of the seasons. So, in a way, I started to lose her even before she left. When the opportunity to escape arose, I suspect that Pixie was glad of the war. Seeing only chance, she was drawn away from us by what we could never offer her; the promise of the unknown.

Although there was often little to buy, I continued to tread my Tuesday steps to the village. Pixie and I had always made this journey together and now I continued alone, clinging to the edges of every familiar chore, searching for traces of my sister along the way. In my wanderings around my memories, I listened for her voice and her thoughts. I still do. And I search for glimpses of her smile in the face of my daughter.

Sometimes in the village there would be a letter to collect or flour to buy and occasionally there was news of a neighbour returning on leave. Looking back, I can see that our parish was lucky, only one neighbour lost more than one son and more than one family remained intact at the end of it all. That Tuesday, I set off home empty-handed but for a letter, something official in an unfamiliar hand. The breeze brought me the scent of wild garlic and reminded me of the first warm day of the previous year, when Jack, Donald, Pixie and I had all trouped down through the woods to the cove in hope of a swim. So perhaps that is why, instead of retracing my route home, I followed the coastal path out of the village.

The farm was close to the sea, but because of the accompaniment of the summer wind in the trees, it was only on still, leafless winter days that we were able to hear the waves crashing onto the shingle down below. When I turned the final twist in the path, I dropped down into a deep, sheltered walkway where foxgloves soared and buttercups sang. I came out into the sunlight and saw that the tide was rolling in, reaching splayed palms and fingers out to the straggling line of seaweed. I stayed close to the cliffs and walked the breadth of the bay. At the far end, I sat high on the rocks and listened to the lazy slap of the surf. Occasionally the sun illuminated the seabed, heralding a dazzle of unnamed, intangible blues. The space held me that day and I wanted to stop time so that I could remain there, encased in the salt air and warmed by the gentle sun. I looked back up the coast where clouds collided in grey and white with a half-hearted whisper of rain. I thought that if I built a small fire I could outstay any shower. The boys had kept a tin of matches and tinder in a crevice further up the beach. I reached my fingers between the cool slices of rock. It was hidden amongst dried out seaweed and clumps of tightly woven fine grass. I pulled the tin out from its nest and opened it. Inside, there was a piece of paper folded up again and again until it was as small as a stamp. I unfolded it.

'Boo!' That was all that it said.

I rolled my eyes; it was so typical of Jack. I chose some large flat pebbles and built a shelter for my fire on a bed of dry sand. I gathered debris and driftwood and put a match to the tinder. I couldn't get it to catch so I used the note. It flared up and disappeared in solitude but not before I saw the tiny scribbled figure of a pixie surrounded by the flames. It was Pixie who had left the 'Boo' for me and I had burnt it. Daft, I know, but I really felt as if I had set light to Pixie herself. Like some sort of voodoo magic.

The fire had not caught. I took the letter out of my pocket and turned it over and over. I picked at it and found that the envelope was double thickness on one side so that I could have enough paper for my needs without revealing the contents. I tore a layer of envelope into four pieces, crumpled them up and set them evenly throughout the fire. I lit one piece and the breeze conspired with me, drawing the shallow flames across the makeshift grate. By the time the rain clouds were overhead and the first drops fell, the fire was well established. I listened as each large drop hit hot stone, sizzled and vanished. The warmth from the fire was such that it was some time before I realised that the side of me facing away from it was soaked. I remember that I did not want to go home but the rain was heavy and wasn't about to shift.

I walked up the path, through the fields and three sets of gates to Falling Meadow. My feet were bare but for the traces of sand, mud and grass on their soles. I carried my shoes and they filled up with water. Rain dripped through my eyelashes and from the end of my nose. I was out of breath when I reached the meadow. I clambered up the slope, clinging to a border scattered with campion and the last of the bluebells. I can't recall being that wet, out of water, before or since. Then I remembered the letter. I stopped under a horse chestnut tree and pulled apart the wet fabric of my pocket. I thought that if I moved the letter now it would fall to pieces. I should wait until the rain stopped, take off my skirt and dry it off in the sun. I stood up to wait so as not to damage the letter further. The sky looked hopeful; there were even patches of blue. I took off my skirt and squeezed out what water I could and left it on the hedge to drip. The sun broke through, pouring down to the earth in heavy, colossal rays. Then the rain stopped and Falling Meadow steamed.

The letter had borne up to its trials better than I had hoped. To prevent the sheets sticking together as they dried out, I resolved to open the letter and set it out in the sun, but on no account to read it. After all, it was addressed to my father. This I did and I sat for an hour or so, beside the letter, just watching the clouds disperse. I looked sideways down at the letter. I put my skirt back on; it didn't seem proper to read a letter from a stranger in just my petticoat.

The content seemed to reach me before my eyes could form the letters and order the words. She had been killed in the aftermath of an air raid, trying to put out a fire. I hugged my knees into me, clenching my fists and crushing the letter. I remember my nails broke the skin of my palms and the pain was not nearly enough.

Inside my tightly closed eyelids, I could see that little pixie, sketched onto the corner of the note, vanishing into the flames.

Red Dahlias

Nina Schmeider

The shrill cry of the peacock sliced the hot, still air of the monsoon month, like the *kirpan*[1] through the soft flesh of a thigh. The barely-there breeze did its best to move the twining bougainvilleas on mud-plastered, ochre-coloured, outside walls of the hut, on which she had painted swirling vines and dancing peacocks with white rice powder. The jasmine bush on one side was starting to turn brown. She raised her eyes heavenward, looking for the rain clouds, and hummed, '*Megha re, Megha…*'

She prayed to the Cloud Gods to bring the rains. The rain songs, part of the ancient Ragas, still invoked deep passions in the hearts of her people. She, like the people of her beloved India, had a lifelong love affair with the rains.

Then she felt the sprinkles on her closed lids. She breathed in deeply, the smell of water on… terracotta?

'Excuse me, ma'am. You will get wet sitting here…' said a voice in English.

'*Satya nash…*' she muttered, opening her eyes reluctantly. She smiled, knowing it wasn't the young man's fault that he happened to be working in the garden centre that had the largest collection of bougainvilleas and jasmine plants. How was he supposed to know that this crazy old Indian woman liked to come and sit on a bench, hidden by tall plants and pretend she was in a hut thousands of miles away. Didn't the old crone have a home?

He was too young to know that sometimes having a home with everything in it didn't prevent people from being homeless.

No it wasn't the fault of this nice young *gora* man. So Mausi gave him one of her toothless smiles, gathered her sari about her and waddled out.

Early next morning Mausi was watering her garden, like she did every day. She had been in this house in Southall for almost five years. Like a dandelion, Southall, populated mostly with people from India, had taken root in this orderly country of *Villayet*. For most of the people who lived here, it was as close as they were ever going to get in this lifetime, to the country they still called home.

Mausi was thinking of the garden centre she had visited the day before, mourning the fact that she couldn't grow bougainvillea in her garden, the way it should be grown: in the soil. The climate was too cold, she had been told. She had seen a pathetic looking bougainvillea in Anita's house once. It had four pale pink flowers on it. A bougainvillea has no claim to the name, if all it has is four pale pink flowers. That's what Mausi thought.

'Why don't you put it in the garden?' she had asked Anita.

'It will die out there...' Anita had said sighing. The girl was always sighing. In her uniform of seasonless heavy silk suits with high necklines, long sleeves and 22 carat jewellery, Anita always looked like a *crore*[2] Rupees. She had a good man, who didn't beat her and paid all the bills for her glittery clothes and gold jewellery. What more could she want?

But the soil here *was* cold.

'Not like my India, where the poor and the homeless can eat the sun's light and heat with a dry *roti,* and still live…' Mausi said to herself. Five years in this country and not a day went by when she didn't miss home.

The garden centre here was the closest she ever came to revisiting her garden in the village. Over the years she had managed to coax some *Angrezi* flowers, the names of which she could never remember: except dahlias. She was on first name basis with the dahlias. The pink fragile-petaled ones were Renus; the small white pompoms were Bobbys, energetic like Anita's boys; and the thin, emaciated stalks with no flowers, were Anitas. Mausi called the red dahlia plants Anita, because, like the girl next door, they were arrogant, shameless self-promoters. It was like they were always saying, 'Look at me. Look at me.'

Mausi never fertilised or dusted the red dahlia plants. And if a stubborn bud dared to poke its head out, Mausi would get her shears and go 'snip' and that would be the end of the upstart.

Why didn't she simply dig them out? Asked Renu once. And she got a glare and a 'No gardener ever throws anything out.' So the red dahlias stayed redless in Mausi's garden.

'*Khasama-noo-khanne.*'

She muttered her favorite swear word, under her breath, as she yanked off the strong root of a dandelion that had put up a good fight but lost. It was no match for Mausi's commitment to a weed-free garden. Then she picked up the hose again.

'There you go, Anita, *bahen ji,*' she said as she directed

a playful stream of water on the only plants in the garden that didn't have any blooms.

She hummed under her breath as the stream of water bathed the dancing leaves and ran around their roots in playful darts. Some of the water trickled down the front of her sari.

'*Satya nash.*' That was Mausi's second favourite swear word.

She heard Renu Ved's voice before she saw her waving at her.

'Mausi. Eh, Mausi,' Renu's voice could have been heard a block away although the Ved house was only across the road. The Veds had moved here only a few months back. Renu was a sweet girl who knew how to treat her elders. Mausi liked Renu.

'*Es...slow...aree...es...slow,*' said Mausi, using up some of her meagre store of English words, putting down the hose, its self-regulating nozzle trickling down to small drops and then dying completely. She knew that Renu understood Punjabi, but Mausi liked to practise her English whenever she could. After all she had been in *Villayet* for five years now and when she went back to her village, people would expect her to say some words in *Angrezi*.

'*Ha...an Putar,*' she said to Renu, happily reverting back to Punjabi, as she crossed the street.

'Mausi, come have some *chai* and *pakoras*. You have been working for hours.' Renu had already cooked breakfast and fed her husband and kids. Now that they were all gone, all busy doing whatever they did everyday of their lives that didn't include her, Renu was doing what she always did when she was alone. She craved company. Especially of someone who would let her make believe, even for a few moments, that she was back in her village.

'Come, come,' she said leading the back way to the kitchen, which was fragrant with the smell of cardamoms and frying oil.

Mausi took off her shoes and put them on one side of the wall and then with a sigh she flopped down on a small settee pushed against the wall. She hated sitting at the black dining table and chairs, with their ramrod straight backs and thin cushions.

'I will sit here,' she said to Renu, pulling up her legs and tucking them under her thighs.

Her age allowed her certain privileges. Although she was an old woman and had no family of her own, she was called Mausi, and treated as a loving aunt by everyone. She played the part of many a loving mother and grandmother to people who had lost their own: not to death but to distance.

Renu put a plate of *pakoras* on the small black lacquered coffee table and two mugs of steaming *chai*. Then there was the usual chitchat of the last week's events. What the children did at school, what Mr Ved said when he saw Renu's paintings. (It was not what he said, but how he said it, said Renu, dabbing at her eyes.) Renu pulled herself together with an effort. For Renu, Mausi was the mother she hadn't seen in more than ten years.

'Tell me about yourself, Mausi. And what's happening over there?' she said gesturing with her eyebrow towards the Sandhu house, Mausi's neighbours.

Jagjit Singh Sandhu had moved to the neighbourhood almost a year ago and still no one knew too much about them except that he was as charitable as he was rich. His wife, Anita, had followed, straight from her village, a few months later, bringing the two little boys with her. A quiet little thing, she never accepted or returned invitations to *chai* or chat from the neighbours and always looked like she was walking in to a dust storm; her eyes scrunched up and her nose wrinkled.

'*Arey Beta*, she is one of those women who are never happy. She is just too arrogant,' Mausi said, remembering the one time she had tried to talk to Anita about the unsuitability of long sleeves in the hot humid English summer. Anita had abruptly turned around and walked away.

Soon it was time for Mausi to head home and cook her lunch. Walking into her yard, she noticed the Sandhus' yard was unusually quiet. Where, she wondered, were those noisy, bratty, adorable little boys? Sometimes the boys snuck into her yard. She would give them *laddoos* and milk with almonds. Almonds are good to make a boy's *danda*³ grow.

She wondered where they were. She noticed Anita's small car wasn't there either. Come to think of it, she hadn't seen them since yesterday evening. She stood watching the Sandhu house for a couple of minutes, then put the hose away on the wall, and headed inside.

She smiled to herself, as she cooked, humming the rain song. It would be just about monsoon season back home. The crows would be sitting on the low walls encircling the flat roofs, cawing for any leftovers.

'*Megha re…Megha…*'

She sang. Then she heard the door.

'*Oye Badmashoo*, in the kitchen. I have something for you…' she called out.

Expecting to hear scrambling feet, and the pushing and shoving arms of the boys rushing in, she was surprised to see it was Sardar ji, Anita's husband, who walked in. A very different Sardar ji than Mausi had ever seen. Every line in his face seemed to be etched in by an artist with an unsteady hand, every hair of his beard trembling with emotion. His eyes were those of a cow with a stillborn calf.

She did what women have always done when faced with people in pain: feed them.

'*Beta, roti* is ready. Eat.'

Sardar ji didn't say anything. He just stared out of the window into the backyard.

'*Beta*, when is she bringing the boys back?' Mausi always called Anita 'she'.

She was stunned when Sardar ji, put his head in his hands and started sobbing. Like all good Indian women, Mausi had been brought up to count on two things in a man: they were never wrong, and they never cried. She looked at Sardar ji. His shoulders shook, his breath whistled through broken sobs, and every now then he would utter, '*Waheguru… Waheguru, forgive this sinner…*'

Now Mausi was scared. She put her hand on his shoulder and said, '*Kaka*, by the grace of *Waheguru*, everything will be all right.'

Sardar ji got up and walked to the back door. He wiped his eyes on the sleeve of his *kurta*, itched his crotch, and cleared his throat. Then he gathered up the bitter poison in his heart in a ball of spit, and sent a stream of it out of the back door.

Then he told her why Anita and the boys wouldn't be coming home.

ooooo

Next day, early in the morning, there was a knock and when Mausi opened it was Sardar ji with the sickly bougainvillea.

'I don't know what to do with it…' he mumbled, and put it down beside her front door and was gone. It was root bound for sure, said Mausi to herself, trying to loosen the soil around the roots. That's when she found it. Wrapped in a plastic bag, a diary, waiting to tell her what she didn't want to know.

For the next few days, Mausi didn't go out at all. She sat in her rocking chair, on the porch, reading and thinking. And reading and thinking some more, till she couldn't read anymore. Then she just did the thinking. She knew now that Anita hadn't wanted much at all and why she wore long sleeves even in the summer. That evening she buried the diary under the red-less dahlia bushes. That was the proper place for it.

During the next few days, Mausi tried to do her usual rounds but her heart wasn't in it. She went for *chai* and *pakoras* to Soma's house and then to Rani's house. Every one was in shock, horror filling in the gaps in their thoughts. She heard only fragments of conversations, voices that would float away in the middle. Snatches of, 'What made her jump? And with her kids too. How could she do that to her kids?' And, 'It was the 5.45 from London, wasn't it?' And then once she heard, 'Isn't that the train Sardar ji always takes on his way back? Oh how awful for him to find out that way…'

Someone mentioned how the news must have rocked the small simple world of Anita's village. The next half an hour was spent debating the superlative qualities of one village over the others. Many a tear was wiped, sobs smothered and sighs silenced as the women consoled each other for the loss of their homes for this cold-blooded *Pardes*.[4]

'*Chup*[5] *bewakoofoo*[6],' Mausi's stern voice momentarily stunned everyone to silence. Slowly she pulled herself off the settee, muttering and shaking her head, she headed for the door. 'I am the biggest *bewakoof*. I should have known. I should have. If only I hadn't been feeling so sorry for myself…'

Mr Ved, coming home from his office that evening, noticed that although it was almost dark, Mausi was still working in the garden. When he mentioned it to Renu, she thought it strange. What was stranger was *where* Mausi was working. With her nose pressed to the glass, Renu watched Mausi feverishly dig the earth around the red dahlias, and then drag the bucket with fertiliser over to the sickly bushes and sprinkle handfuls at the roots. All the while, the old lady kept talking to herself and gesturing. What on earth was she doing? Finally Renu couldn't stand it any more.

'Mausi, eh Mausi, what are you doing to the red dahlias?' yelled Renu from her porch. 'They are brown and sickly, they will never flower, you know.'

Mausi stopped for a moment and looked at Renu and then up and down the street at happy windows, clouded with loud and busy lives. Except for one.

'They will have the biggest blooms. Just you wait, ha…an,' Mausi's voice was loud enough for everyone to hear, even inside their cotton-woolled, spice-aired houses. 'They just needed to be talked to…Ha…an ji, that's all they need. You'll see.'

'But…but, they are red,' spluttered Renu.

'They shall be, *Waheguru* willing, they shall be,' said Mausi as she went back to work.

Next morning, before any of the neighbors were up, Mausi dragged the pot with bougainvillea out to the front yard, took it out of the pot.

'*Haey Ram*… you poor thing…' she spat on the ground. Then right beside her front door to the right, she dug a hole deep enough, put some fertiliser in it, and planted the bougainvillea. After giving it some water and tying the fragile stalks to the stakes behind, Mausi got down to the serious business of having a heart-to-heart.

'*Arey*, look here, *bahena*. Here's the deal. I will water you and fertilise you and talk to you every day. In the winter I will wrap you in burlap and keep you warm. All you have to do is put down roots. You think you can do that, *ha…an?*'

Then she sat down in her rocking chair and looked up at the sky and thought, 'The Monsoons should be here any day now…' She sat and rocked and hummed: '*Megha re Megha…*'

Footnotes:
[1] Ceremonial dagger
[2] Ten million
[3] Stick. Also slang for penis
[4] Foreign land
[5] Quiet
[6] Fools

Councillor Abraham's Growing Concern

Ally Thomas

As Victor Abraham slid the agenda into his briefcase, a removal van pulled up at the house next door followed immediately by a matt-finished orange saloon. As it parked up, the rear passenger door fell into the road. Victor had planned on introducing himself properly to his new neighbour, in his capacity as both Neighbourhood Watch co-ordinator and community councillor, but this rather spoilt the tone. Victor frowned and hoped it would be attended to immediately or he would have complaints. He checked his pens in his top pocket, closed the front door behind him, and straightened up the matching urns of clipped *Buxus*.

What furniture he could see, in passing, was covered in plastic against the dreary March drizzle. A woman stood at one side of the front door, shielding her fading titian hair with a frilly umbrella.

'Good Morning,' he nodded as he passed.

'Sod all good about it, luvvy.'

Victor winced.

'Mind your back, mate.'

'Less you want to be carted in and all, mate.'

Victor hurried down the street. Next door had been empty since old Mrs Brown had died. He'd heard on the grapevine that her daughter was moving in, but nobody had seen her in years. 'Luvvy' indeed! Perhaps this woman

135

was the housekeeper or the cleaner. He opened the door to the village hall where the rest of the committee, already seated, stopped chatting abruptly. Had he got the time wrong, he wondered?

The Chair went through the usual apologies and minutes and then bumbled into the agenda: 'Swanford in Bloom.' There was a general murmuring of interest.

'This year, in addition to best formal front garden display and best hanging basket arrangement, it is proposed we introduce a best street category.'

'Seconded,' Victor said, crossing his arms and smiling. Joan, sitting opposite, rolled her eyes heavenward.

'You don't approve, Joan?'

'Not at all, Victor. It's just some people…you know… are not gardeners and you know how you…'

'Seconded.'

The motion was carried and Victor mentally checklisted his neighbours. He had won the formal display himself last year and was sure that with a little gentle encouragement they would all step up to the mark. Actually, now that he thought of it, it was a perfect way of introducing himself properly to his newest neighbour without her assuming he had any personal interest.

Arabella Fallabella popped a cork and poured champagne into a mug – from which she swigged as she unpacked her clothes into a single canvas wardrobe. She had always travelled light; always the less the better. There was a knock at her front door. She looked down from the window to see, squinting up, the same short middle-aged man who had greeted her earlier.

'Come in. Come on in and let's get a look at you.'

'No, no. Thank you, I'll wait down here, you must be busy with the…er…move. But I wondered if you'd be interested in details of the "Swanford in Bloom" community garden competition?'

She thrust her head out of the window.

'I simply can't wait to get started, lover. First garden I've ever had. Beside a bottle garden that is. Will you take a drink with me?'

'No, I… It's a little early for me,' his eyes took in the depth of her bosom, 'but welcome to the street and I… I'll drop a leaflet into you later on. It's only March after all. Plenty of time for planning the street display.'

'Planning?' Arabella looked at him with her head tilted to the left, inviting a response.

Victor shook his head as he turned in at his gate. Bottle garden. Bottle garden? Victor didn't bother his neighbour for some time after that, in fact, not until the day that the postman wrongly delivered a sheaf of seed catalogues. He took them over to her and she positively lunged for them.

'Cheers, Vic. Nothing like a bit of plant porn.'

'No. No. Indeed. I er…must er…go. Dusting.'

He was sure he heard her laughing as he cleaned the leaves of his daffodils.

'So, I can put you down for two dozen geraniums, red, three trays of *Alyssum*, white, and three trays of *Lobelia*, standard blue. They'll be delivered once the frosts have passed,' Victor told old Fred. He tapped his pad with his pencil in satisfaction as he strode up the road.

Victor had found that he could get a discount from the Swanford Gardening Society if he ordered in bulk and he was sure that Miss Fallabella would oblige with a few more, to make up the order, and rather conveniently there she was outside, taking a large delivery.

Must be a sofa…but it was huge. Where the hell was she going to put it? Two men struggled with its bulk in the weak sunshine while Victor totted up the order and walked further along the crescent to try the Fforbeses. The thing was monstrous, the size of a swingboat.

After lunch he was eventually tempted to peek over the garden fence. Miss Fallabella was in the back garden. She was facing away from him and bending over. She appeared to be trowelling away at the soil. He cleared his throat.

'What do you think?' she asked, waving vaguely at the enormous orange and yellow fibreglass canopy that now sheltered her kitchen window. 'Someone told me that these gardens are suntraps. Thought I'd need some shade…or somewhere to look at the stars from.'

'Very nice I'm sure, but it's not really quite in-keeping with the general—'

'Mr Abraham. Let's get this straight. We're not all the same, you know. For example, I imagine you spend quite a lot of time with your head stuck up your own behind?'

'Miss Fallabella. I'm really not sure what you mean. I only wanted to offer to order some plants for you, from the garden society. Your late mother liked a few neat tubs about the place.'

'I last saw my mother when I was seventeen years of age. What influence she ever had over me has long since buggered off, Vic.'

He cringed then dropped back to his own garden as if struck by a stone.

That evening Victor scanned his copy of the local planning regulations. Did the canopy rob his light? No. Was it likely to cause a danger to traffic? No. Did it obstruct a footpath? No. He ground his teeth until his jaw ached, remembered her, bent forward over the border, and flung the regulations to the floor.

When her car pulled up outside on Saturday it resembled a mobile triffid. Leaves and tendrils spilled out of the windows and the boot was propped open, some root-balled fig trees sitting sedately amongst the riot. Victor was kneeling on a pad of foam on his front path. He had already planted one white *Ageratum* 'Swiss Timing' and now, ruler in hand, was measuring where to dig the next hole. He tried not to look up.

'Morning, my dear.'

He didn't reply.

'Now don't go worrying about me, Vic. I've got a few plants in myself. I've maxed me card out with this little lot. What a show we'll have.'

He straightened up, rubbing his back and wondering what she wanted him to say.

'Have you settled on a colour scheme, Miss Fallabella? I find that's the biggest mistake with novice gardeners, you need a bit of a theme to keep a sense of cont—"

'You can call me Arabella, Vic. I thought…Yellow. Orange. Red. Pink. Sensational.'

Victor thought back to that last committee meeting.

Val had obviously known all about her. All of them. They must all have been loving it, rubbing their hands in anticipation of his discomfort. Knowing he wouldn't stand a chance of getting first this year. Not with her next door. He felt his complexion reddening, and a weird, burning confusion. She wore little sandals and she kept extending her toes, pointing them at him.

He cleared his throat. 'Six inches,' he muttered.

'Come again?'

'Six inches. Between each plant. That's what it says in the book.'

That evening, Victor was standing at the bottom of the garden, checking the temperature of his compost heap. Although he had tried to stop himself, his eyes were drawn to Arabella's house. She definitely needed blinds at the back windows, he could see her quite plainly. As if she was looking in to a mirror, she undid the cord of her dressing gown and the sides fell away. She smoothed her hands down over her waist and hips and tweaked the back of her figure-hugging costume from between her buttocks and then, looking somewhat satisfied, she turned away.

By eight a.m. the next morning, despite having to do some extensive weeding as some rather exotic looking plantlets had started to colonise his front garden, Victor had finished his design. It was an exact replica of the town's floral clock. After baiting it heavily against slugs, he sat with his cup of decaffeinated and his copy of the *Express* at the patio table. He applied himself diligently to the crossword and was doing quite well, despite the fact that Arabella had been singing out of tune all the while from the other side of the fence. She stopped momentarily.

'*Clematis tangutica* – orange peel blooms; where, oh where, oh where… Let's find the perfect spot for you, mmhm?' The trowel clattered against stone. 'Gazanias; ooh look at you funny boys. Zig-zagging all over your faces.'

Victor mistook three down for three across, cursed quietly and applied correcting fluid.

'African marigolds…Naughty Marietta…*Clematis montana*…'

Victor's ears swivelled. Anything '*montana*' meant 'rampant' and she was planting it next to his fence panels. If it dared… If it dared to even extend one curling tendril onto his property he would snip it off and hand it back to her with pleasure.

A low rumble at nine announced the arrival of yet another delivery lorry. He busied himself in a border while affording himself an angle from where he could still see what was going on. Pretending to hoe, he was alarmed to spot some more familiar little leaf shapes. He was sure they were nasturtiums, garish silly clowns that drew blackfly like nothing else.

'Yooooohoooo,' Arabella ran through to her front door, trailing soil behind her. Two burly guys checked her address carefully and then carried their cargo straight through the house and out into the garden.

'Where do you want them?'

'Stack them against the house, please, then come in. I've got the kettle on. You got the cement mixer, lads?'

Victor's ears jerked. Permanent foundations. There

were regulations on sheds.

On the way to the civic centre he noticed that the slugs had had a go at his *Alyssum* and the local ginger tom had dug up the little hand of the clock. He drove down the road noting a person of restricted growth walking along.

When he got home, armed with sheaves of documents, he went straight up to his bedroom and peered down into *her* garden. But there was no shed, only a pair of shiny black line posts. The posts were very tall and very close together. Altogether too close, you wouldn't get many towels on that length of line. People these days mostly preferred rotary lines. Radio masts? If she didn't have a licence he could get her for that. He noticed how her borders were filling out. The first trumpetings from the lily pots sounded, the *tangutica* tumbled over a pretty pergola and peppery nasturtiums coughed from every crevice. So that's where they were coming— Suddenly she was outside and looking straight at him, he stepped behind the curtain and covered his face with his hand.

The envelope decorating his doormat at teatime left a little trail of glitter and sequins as he picked it up. The writing whooped and whirled and at first he thought it was a mistake, some childish prank.

Miss Arabella Fallabella, of number twenty- two Jubilee Crescent, requests the company of Mr Victor Abraham at her Garden Warming Party. Tomorrow. Time 7.30pm Bring yourself. Bring a bottle. Bring a chair.

He read it again. A chair? The woman was insane. Bottles yes, chairs no. It was bound to get out of hand. No, he would sit indoors and monitor it just in case a noise abatement order was merited. He tucked the invitation into the letter rack. At twilight he turned on the outside tap and began watering his perfect ranks, counting as he delivered exactly the same seconds-worth of water to each plant.

The evening was still and heavily perfumed. A sudden coolness travelled over him almost like a solar eclipse as the air was disturbed. He turned towards *her* garden and then staggered back as a sudden vertigo unbalanced him. Miss Arabella was sat on a bar, high up in the air, swooshing through the tops of the black poles. She jerked back and then swung forward powerfully but with effortless grace.

She was wearing a scarlet sequinned leotard that clung to her full bosom and tights that hugged at her thighs, an aerial artiste… She let go of one rope and flung a scattering of something into his garden. Her instep arched so perfectly that he thought his heart would flick-flack out from his chest. She leant backwards until she hung upside down, her hair like a lion's mane around her head.

Swallows flitted over her, bats registered her and adjusted their course. Victor's trouser turn-ups darkened as they soaked up the water as his hose made a pool on the path. He took off his shoes as he went indoors, tore up the planning regulations and got out the invitation. He could barely fill out the RSVP for the trembling of his fingers.

On the evening of the party, Victor showered, dressed, dabbed on some 'Old Spice' and listened to the convoy of vehicles pulling up outside. It was an odd selection of customised vans and lorries. There was even a tiny pony grazing on the service strip outside his front door. The person of restricted growth was offering it water, which it drank freely. Its silver grey flanks were shining and fleetingly Victor ran the livestock byelaws through his mind then cursed himself. The pony drifted in through his gate and started on the floral clock and he really didn't care. He felt as if he was trapped in a dream that she had conjured up. He had watched her buttocks sat on the bar, her warm, strong limbs…

He carried his chair in front of him as he walked up to her door and knocked.

A man with a waxed moustache, dressed in a leopard-skin loincloth, opened the door.

'Miss Arabella, Miss Arabella, he's here.' People were balanced on the arms of chairs juggling drinks and popcorn, toffee apples and melting ice cream but he was ushered through by many pairs of hands.

'Victor. Out here. Victor…' Arabella commanded. 'Oh good, you've brought your chair. Victor, you have a ringside seat.'

Victor sat down and watched, mesmerised, as she climbed the pole and readied herself to push out from the little platform and into the evening air.

'I never thought…I never dreamed…'

'Watch me, Victor, watch me fly.'

The garden burst into applause.

Hortus Conclusus

Imogen Rhia Herrad

It was like an island in the horribleness of life. Green, full of colour, filled with flowers and with beauty. Little flowers were hiding beneath the larger ones. Some had round faces and open petals like hands held palms outwards. There were flowers hung like bells from a curved stem. Others curled, bashfully, inwards, hiding their faces. She didn't like those, they reminded her too much of herself.

'We're going to have to talk, you and I,' her mum would say, and open the door to the stuffy sitting room no one ever sat in. Her stomach would feel as though it was full of lead and broken glass, and she would have to make her legs move and walk along the corridor and over the threshold and into the room, and then the door would shut and she would be inside with no escape.

The walls were full of framed pictures behind glass. The window was hidden behind a waterfall of net curtain. Her mum stood in front of the door. No escape.

She had to listen while her mum talked about all the bad things she had done. The things that were wrong about her. Her lying. The schoolwork that was never good enough. The dirt she brought into the house, the noise she made, her lack of consideration for others, her selfishness.

She would stand and listen and feel her shoulders droop and her face go wooden with the effort not to cry, because her mum didn't like it when she cried. Her insides felt empty, now, as though she had been scraped out like a slaughtered pig, the way she'd once seen it done on the farm next door. Only the pig had been dead and it hadn't cared what happened to its insides.

Her mum's voice felt like needles, like a fork piercing her ears, her eyes, her skin. No way out.

Then one day she had looked around the room out of the corners of her eyes, slyly, like an animal trapped and looking for escape. And had seen the garden for the first time, filled with colours and beauty, an island in the horribleness of life. She didn't know the names for all the flowers, but some she recognised – camomile: white and yellow with dark green leaves; creamy lilies-of-the-valley, blazing bluebells, golden daffodils, daisies hiding in the grass, looking skywards. Rabbits were running and playing amongst the flowers and under the two small trees, an oak and a holly.

While she was being talked to she would look at the garden, concentrate with all her might on one flower, study it intently. First, the petals. One. Then another. And another. The round, cushiony bit in the middle, like a coin or a face. And finally, the stem and the leaves. All as slowly as she could. She would only allow herself one plant at a time.

When her Mum had finished talking and it was time for her to pull up her skirt and receive the punishment, she held on fast to the flowers and the colours and the rabbits running free.

She would imagine tearing herself loose from the iron hand on her thigh, the lashing hand on her buttocks. Running across the polished floorboards, treacherous as ice, and flinging herself forwards, at just the right angle to pass through the magical doorway and into the garden.

And there she would live, safe from the world, and never have to come out again.

When people asked about her childhood, she'd roll her eyes and laugh with the corners of her mouth turned down. 'Don't ask.' Over the years she had perfected the gesture, the tone of voice, the self-mocking grimace. Nothing worth knowing, they said, really, nothing happened in my life.

And it was nobody's business, anyway.

She did her work well. She was thorough and clever and quick. She laughed at things nobody else found funny, always with the corners of her mouth pulled down and her eyebrows raised. Not much went past her. She wasn't greatly liked, but she was respected.

It was how she preferred it.

She lived well enough. Her job paid a reasonable salary and was not unpleasant. Of course, her being only a secretary was a bit of a disappointment. She knew that her mum had expected more of her. But after she had finished school, she hadn't really felt like going on to university, spending more time sitting and listening. She'd wanted to do something, and more than anything she wanted to do something with her hands. Ideally, she would have trained as a carver or a potter or a goldsmith, somebody who made things. But her mum wouldn't have it, and she hadn't felt like making a big thing of it, and an argument, and putting her mum out. She didn't know any other girls who wanted to do that sort of thing for a living. Maybe if she had, she could have said, Look – Sally, or Cathryn, or Nesta, is training as a goldsmith; why can't I then? But there wasn't anyone else like her, and so that was that. She'd compromised and gone to work for a law firm instead that still took on trainees for clerical jobs, and now at thirty-seven she was a senior secretary, and it wasn't so bad.

She had her own flat, and although it was a bit dark, she could at least afford the mortgage, and there were worse places. The trick with life was not to ask too much.

She had friends, but not many, and she didn't see them often. She found people exhausting. Her life was well organised and predictable. It was only in her dreams that chaos burst through.

Every now and again she would wake up with the sheets in a tangle. Her eyes would be swollen as though she'd cried in her sleep, although she never cried; and her mind was full of mad disordered images: moonlight and flowers on a red meadow, big cats on the prowl and rabbits playing and a beautiful woman who looked like no one she'd ever seen. On those mornings after the dream she felt heavy and sullen, disorientated and sad. It baffled her, because she had no reason to be sad.

The images would follow her all through the day. She would catch herself staring out of the window or at her computer screen, looking at nothing, while her mind's eye tried to piece together the red meadow strewn with wild flowers, the lion, the woman. She tried to see the place again with the clarity it had possessed in her dream, not the fragments that were all she had left upon waking. She longed for the red meadow, and it frightened her. She didn't understand its meaning.

I'm homesick for it, she thought one day; but that didn't

make sense either. There hadn't been a garden at home, it had been concreted over, her mum had said it was tidier that way. And anyway, she thought, stopping that train of thought, her mum was dead and the house sold, and there was nothing to be homesick for.

When they told her about the day out, she wasn't going to go. She hated office parties.

'But this isn't a party,' said the woman who was leaving, one of the junior partners. 'I don't like parties either, that's why I want to go to the exhibition instead. You won't even have to talk.' She'd said it with a wink that almost took the sting out of her words. 'Come on. We're all going. I'd like you to come.'

She knew that people didn't much care for her. Somehow, this direct invitation disarmed her. She rolled her eyes, grinned, sighed an exaggerated sigh. 'Oh, all right then. If I must.'

They arrived at the museum in three taxis. Apart from the senior partners, the entire office had come. She hated it, the laughter, the voices, the physical proximity. She should never have come. The old pain in her thigh came back, sharp as a steel vice. It always did in moments of stress. She'd had it checked but there was nothing physically wrong that anyone could find.

She clenched her teeth, determined to get away as soon as she could, and walked to the entrance, trying not to limp.

And there it was. She stopped dead at the entrance to the first exhibition room. A red meadow, strewn with flowers, encircling a smaller patch of green, like an island.

A woman sat in the centre of the green, stroking a unicorn. At her side sat a lion, and rabbits ran and played in the grass and a small leopard walked about.

'The *hortus conclusus*,' a guide's voice said at her side, 'the enclosed garden, is a common motif in mediaeval art. It was perceived as a tranquil place and a safe space into which to withdraw, a refuge from the chaos of the world outside. The unicorn represents…'

A green island in a sea of red. Beauty as a refuge from the world. Blazing bluebells, creamy lilies-of-the-valley, camomiles white and yellow with dark green leaves, golden daffodils, daisies looking skywards underneath an oak and a holly tree.

A tapestry. A garden on a tapestry.

She swayed and walked on unsteady feet to a bench.

'The Lady and the Unicorn,' said the woman whose leaving do this was, and sighed happily. 'Isn't it beautiful? I've always wanted to see this.'

'We had one at home,' she heard herself say. 'A print, of course. In the sitting room.'

She hadn't thought of the sitting room in years. She'd forgotten that there had been a sitting room at home. She knew that there had been a house, stairs and corridors and rooms, but she'd forgotten what they looked like. She remembered the window of her own room, and looking out of it, but she couldn't have said what colour the walls had been.

But there was the sitting room now. She could look back into the past and see it as clear as a photo, the brown varnished door, the net-curtained window, the walls with their yellowing wallpaper which her mum had never changed after her dad's death, the mirror over the mantelpiece, the framed pictures on the walls. The pictures had mostly been old, dark, oil paintings, all except for the one that showed a green patch of garden surrounded by red, all of it covered in a multitude of flowers… Riotous, chaotic flowers, beautiful and alive in all that deadness.

She remembered the flowers more than anything. She looked at them now, and the pain in her thigh flared up, sharp and cruel like a hand clawing her leg and not letting go. Her mum's voice, listing all the things that were bad and wrong about her. The flowers, the colours, the rabbits running free. The hand lashing out at her. Until one day she had found a way out of the sitting room, and through the red and over the wall and into the garden: And there she had stayed, safe from the world, and had never come back out again.

She left the museum. She knew that she should have said goodbye, but she couldn't wait. She took her childhood self by the hand and together they ran out of the building and down the steps and into the streets of the town.

There was a flower shop in her road. She'd never been in there before. She had meant to clean up the rubbish-strewn strip of soil beyond her kitchen door, which the estate agent had referred to as 'the garden', but she'd never got round to it in all the years she'd lived in the flat. Now, she went into the shop and bought every kind of seed packet they had, and a spade, and gloves for her hands.

She was going to make a garden for herself, green with grass and filled with flowers, and colour, and beauty.

The Brilliant Blue Delphiniums

Elizabeth Morgan

At last they were planted, fifteen brilliant blue delphiniums. The garden faced south, and always had its maximum share of sun, but this corner of the herbaceous border and lawn was a veritable suntrap, where on summer evenings, the sun's rays would squeeze into those ten square metres of garden until the last ounce of warm pink light had been drained from them. For George and his wife Amelia it had been the perfect spot to construct the pergola, on a carefully contoured patio, furnished appropriately with table, chairs and sunloungers.

Although over recent years Britain seemed to be having warmer summers, it could never be relied upon, and so George always felt that the very presence of sunloungers served as a meteorological nudge. And now the brilliant blue delphiniums would provide a visual feast even on a dull day. When they grew, of course, for at the moment, they were no more than three inches high.

George rose from the flowerbed somewhat stiffly, straightened his back, dabbed his damp top lip, and looked at his new watch. How odd, he thought, to be in the garden at eleven o'clock, today of all days, the start of the new term. Under normal circumstances, he would have been in the sixth form Common Room discussing curricula and careers with the brightest high flyers. But that was another life…

George had been a teacher at the town's prestigious boys' public school for more years than he cared to count and had been passionate about teaching, and about his pupils. He had a doctorate in history, had written his thesis on the medieval chroniclers (which had been published as an Open University paperback), had contributed regularly to learned journals, and had even appeared twice on television.

As his tall, lean frame ambled across the lawn towards the house he felt a little pang of nostalgia for the Masters' Common Room, the jokes, the banter, the bonhomie, and the shared pride whenever the school had a record number of places at Oxbridge. Latterly, he had been feeling a little jaded with the world of education, and although the first to admit that in the public school sector they were a protected species, compared with their brethren in the inner cities, he had nevertheless been ready to retire at the end of last term.

Now, at sixty-five, George was eager to concentrate his energies and passions on something other than the classroom and academia. There were many avenues open and available for his intellect and energy, but for the moment life promised to be totally fulfilling thanks to his abiding passion for the garden. There had never been enough time in the past, and others had had to be employed to do much of the work he loved, but now he had all the time in the world.

Each weekend he used to spend hours at the local garden centre, and was a regular visitor to the Chelsea Flower Show. In fact, it had been at the most recent show he had bought the delphiniums – on the last day.

Amelia, George's wife, was a little younger and still

teaching. Although she had not the slightest interest in the upkeep and maintenance of the garden, she appreciated the results of her husband's painstaking colour coordination and balance of flowering plants, planned somewhat obsessively, she thought, to provide interest throughout the year. She loved the undulating borders he had created; they encroached upon the lawn in unexpected shapes, like an incoming tide. George found horticultural symmetry boring, and loved the unexpected. Over the years he had created secret gardens with an abundant variety of plant life in the copse at the far end of the garden that had been hideouts for the children's games, and now were equally loved by their visiting grandchildren. George's other passion was archaeology, and in order to encourage the same in his offspring he had buried all sorts of *objets* in his secret gardens. Once they had even found a coin and several pieces of pottery that hadn't been buried by their father.

Striding back to the house, across the lawn, George made a mental note that the grass needed a centimetre off and the laburnum needed trimming; its fronds were almost trailing in the Japanese water garden.

In the spacious kitchen he put on the kettle for a cup of tea and smiled contentedly. He smiled at the prospect of doing just what he wanted to for the foreseeable future. How lovely life had become. How carefree…

The house was one of a rather select twenty or so, built circa 1910, in a wooded part of the town's outskirts. Solid, large, Edwardian and red brick, the houses were very expensive to buy now, and new arrivals these days tended to be, in George's opinion, *arrivistes* with more money than taste, or even sense, for some had pulled down beautifully moulded walls to create an 'open-plan' effect, and put in replacement windows without any regard to period. There was a discreet pecking order in the 'close', based on who had lived there the longest and whoever had, automatically became leader of the neighbourhood welcoming party. It had fallen to George and Amelia, therefore, to host the drinks party for the newest arrivals, who, a few months ago, had bought the house next door. A middle-aged couple, Shirley and Colin Witherspoon, who, no children in sight, doted on their very large, white, Persian cat (which appeared to take up a great deal of their time, energy and space). Amelia, with her warm, kindly nature, had befriended the Witherspoons and very soon she and Shirley started to invite each other for tea at weekends, when husbands were either in the garden or watching sport on television.

When Amelia returned from school this particular afternoon, she and George strolled round the garden in comfortable silence – except for his comments about the general health of each sprouting bud and twig, not forgetting the new delphiniums. As they were clearing supper, Amelia said, apropos of nothing, 'He really is very beautiful.'

George smirked, 'Who? Colin?'

'No, George, Saladin; the cat.'

'Saladin? I didn't know his name was Saladin. How pretentious.'

'Come on, dear, he is a Persian cat.'

'Saladin wasn't Persian.'

'Well, as Shirley says, it was that neck of the woods.

Anyway, they are having such trouble with him.'

'Why?'

'When they first let him out he got an infected paw, so they're trying to keep him in.'

'He won't like that.'

'Apparently, he's clawing all the furniture, desperate for freedom, but Shirley thinks it could be all right soon. They're taking him to the vet.'

'Putting him down?'

'Don't be silly, George. To see about getting him, you know – done. Curb his wanderlust.'

George grinned. 'Poor little sod.' He tapped his wife playfully on her bottom. 'Glad mine's not about to be curbed.'

Amelia giggled. She was still a pretty woman, although the years had added their pounds of flesh. Like many older married couples, who develop different bedtime habits, she and George had decided, when the children finally left, to take separate bedrooms. George was a bad sleeper and frequently snored when he did. Amelia was a light sleeper who sometimes read into the early hours. So the arrangement suited them both. As for sex, without the call of nature urging them to procreate, and with no one around to bother them, a cuddle on the settee seemed to be a more comfortable and less predictable option than heaving about under the bedclothes. George had the bedroom at the back of the house, with his office and bathroom to hand. From the window he could look out onto the beautiful garden with a frisson of pride – he alone had created this vision. He was a punctilious man. His habits were regular. All those years of timetables and examinations had honed him into a most efficient timekeeper. His new daily regime, based on unlimited freedom, would be just as rigorously structured as before, but, of course, in a different way.

It was Monday, barely two weeks into his new life, and George strode purposefully, as always, into his beloved garden for the morning tour of inspection, armed with a pencil and notebook – in which to jot down tasks for the day. The sun shone, the birds sang and George had never felt so at peace with himself and the world. The blue delphiniums sitting primly in the sunny corner had taken well. He bent down and touched them fondly. They were akin to his babies, and the nearest he would ever come in this world to nurturing new life. A little further down the garden was a small gap in the hedge that separated the house from its neighbour, and as George rose from the flowerbed he perceived a flash of white. Somewhat startled, he crept carefully towards the sighting in order not to disturb whatever it was; perhaps even a wounded creature.

And then he saw him – next door's Persian. For a moment George had completely forgotten about his new neighbour. 'Oh, it's you, Saladin. Don't think you should come in here. Off you go.'

He bent down to stroke the cat. Saladin stood as still as stone and growled.

'Go on, shoo!'

The cat glared, angry, his face puckered into a fierce frown. George clapped his hands loudly.

'Go on, back to your own patch!'

Saladin hissed and sauntered off.

That night, George couldn't sleep. He felt uneasy, about what he had no idea. That is until he looked out of the window, when the early light of dawn was filtering through the garden's foliage. An unmistakeable white shape was prowling across the lawn.

Without a moment's hesitation, George opened the window and hissed loudly: 'Get off my lawn! Go!'

The cat stared up at the open window. With his long bushy tail swaying in the air, he turned slowly and with the same insolence as an adolescent boy sashayed defiantly back to the gap in the hedge.

Rattled and tired, through lack of sleep, George spent the hours before daybreak in the kitchen drinking countless cups of tea, but true to type, began his morning inspection at the scheduled hour. To say he was horrified by the sight that met his weary eyes would be a gross understatement. Two of his precious delphiniums had been uprooted and lay limply on soil that had been savaged. A fox, perhaps? Never one to jump to conclusions without first examining the evidence, George took a closer look at the patch. And there it was. Irrefutable evidence – Saladin had left his calling card.

There were two immediate solutions: to block the gap in the hedge and to replant his two babies on the far edge of the cluster, both of which George executed forthwith.

'Pepper, that will stop him. Always works. Put it where he's – you know. They always go to the same place.'

Following Amelia's advice, the next day George went to the local supermarket and bought a quarter of a pound of white pepper, which he sprinkled liberally onto Saladin's chosen latrine. 'That will teach you – blasted animal!'

George went to bed relaxed, assured that victory was in his pocket. Even if the cat could get into the garden, he would find it pretty uncomfortable squatting in half a pound of pepper.

The next morning, a dumbfounded George picked up the next pair of delphiniums. Not only was Saladin resourceful, he was slowly extending his territory.

Replanting his injured babes on the outer edge of the bed, next to the other *mutilées*, George decided that drastic measures would have to be taken, despite Amelia's friendship with Shirley.

By midday he was filling his new shotgun with pellets. He would catch Saladin as he squatted. The very idea brought a smile to his face.

At 4 am the alarm went off. George leapt out of bed, quietly opened the window and sat watching, like Dylan Thomas' Captain Cat. He was particularly anxious to know how the mighty Saladin had been able to penetrate the garden's defences. Unfortunately, he dozed off at the crucial moment, and woke with a start only to see the white blob cavorting rapturously near the patio. George grabbed his rifle and was so excited that he could barely aim. The shot ripped like a thunderbolt through the tranquil air and the white blob vanished.

A few moments later, George saw that next door's kitchen light had been turned on. This could mean civil war...

The following morning it was brutally clear: the enemy had infiltrated and caused similar destruction yet again, facilitated by the dozing watch. Two more – it was always two – of George's delphinium babes had been wrenched out of their beds and left to die on ravaged soil. Saladin was hell bent upon his latrine building empire...

A melancholy George sat in his study and tried to analyse the problem logically. Although he wanted to strangle the cat, George was a civilised man and therefore there had to be a rational solution. Shirley had already asked if they had heard a shot in the night. Amelia was so embarrassed at having to play the innocent that George's new shotgun was banished forthwith to the loft. If only he could sit in the garden overnight, the cat wouldn't dare come in.

Yes, that was it! That's what scarecrows were all about. Why hadn't he thought about it before?

Two hours later, with the excitement of the truly desperate, George had created a replica of himself made up of several pillows, a ball of string, a pair of trousers, a jacket, a hat and sunglasses. The moment his scarecrow was securely held in place on a deckchair, he felt the thrill of impending victory. It was perfect. Carefully he carried his alter ego out onto the patio, facing the now severely depleted delphinium patch. Aware that Saladin could be sitting watching, his flattened nose pressed tight against one of the many upstairs windows, or be sneaking a peep through the hedge, George chatted away to himself in order to doubly confuse the Persian warrior.

Night fell... For half an hour George kept vigil from his window. All was calm. To be absolutely sure he set the alarm for 4 am, Saladin's witching hour, and waited by the open window. But not for long. The feline wonder somehow wriggled through the seemingly impenetrable hedge, took a few steps towards the delphiniums, spotted the scarecrow and, joy of joys, bolted like lightning back into his own garden. George was jubilant. He could hardly wait to tell Amelia over breakfast.

For three ensuing days the baby delphiniums were left untouched by Saladin. The scarecrow was brilliantly successful. It was during the early hours of the fourth night that George awoke quite suddenly. He sat up in bed and saw that it was 4 am. Despite the surrounding blanket of silence and a somnolent brain, a sixth sense propelled him to the window. He froze in anger. He was flabbergasted: his brain already awash with hideous forms of feline murder. The white blob was at it again!

Saladin was actually taking commando runs at the scarecrow. Between attacks he prowled around the immobile figure at a safe distance, waiting for a reaction. When none came, fired with daring, he took a flying leap at one stuffed leg, then the other and then both arms. Finally, having dismembered his prey and scattered feathers and stuffing over the lawn, the creature leapt triumphantly on what was left of the scarecrow's head tearing at the cap as if it were a chicken leg.

George sat on the bed in despair. What on earth could he do?

The next morning, predictably, two more delphinium babes had been cruelly taken from their beds, and with heavy heart, their sorrowing father replanted them in their ever shifting home.

It took several hours to gather the remains of the scarecrow and its entrails into black plastic bags. By now somewhat concerned for her husband's health and temper, Amelia suggested the delphiniums be transplanted to the opposite side of the patio.

'We'll still be able to see them, George. In fact, we'll be looking straight at them. It's obvious Saladin has taken a fancy to that corner for his – you know what.'

It seemed the only sensible solution.

Throughout the day George transplanted – with tender loving care – both healthy and ailing delphiniums into a carefully prepared new nursery, full of the very best plant nutrients, leaving the old bed completely free for Saladin's king-sized latrine.

But inside, George seethed with anger, his usual forebearance cast aside. 'Who'd have thought a bloody cat could chase us, literally, out of any part of our garden?'

Amelia had never seen him in such *extremis*. He was as much of a cause for concern as the damaged delphiniums. His eyes were red and dark-ringed. He wasn't eating properly and could barely concentrate on the current affairs TV programmes he normally followed with such assiduous interest.

'I mean, where do we go from here?'

'George, dear,' Amelia soothed, 'cats are creatures of habit and always go to the same place. It'll be all right now, you'll see. I'm sure he doesn't want to damage the delphiniums, that's why he's been digging them up and removing them from his loo.' She patted her husband's head affectionately. 'Quite thoughtful, really.'

'Very,' growled George. 'And judging by the size of his property development, he is obviously building a feline community centre! We shall be overrun! Amelia, you'll have to talk to her – to Shirley.'

'Very well, dear, but why not you? You are the only one who knows exactly what the cat gets up to in the early hours.'

'And if I tell her that I tried to shoot the damn thing, what then?'

'No! You couldn't do that. She'd be horrified. They dote on Saladin.'

'I'll give it one last chance, and then it's me or the cat, Amelia. Think about it!' He struck the table hard with the palm of his hand and walked the length of the kitchen, hands in pockets: Gary Cooper in 'High Noon'.

It was becoming a habit now. George woke at 4 am and with sinking heart and bleary eyes crossed to the window. There it was, that detestable white blob playing in the garden.

'Huh, bet that's confused you! No plants! Enough room for you, eh?' he sneered. His fists closed round an imaginary Saladin's neck and squeezed.

The following morning George could hardly believe his eyes. This was the last straw. The cat had found the new bed of baby delphiniums and had uprooted two of them, but this time they were dead, lying on the desecrated soil. Another hole and another latrine, while Saladin's completed community centre lay undisturbed. At eight thirty and unshaven, George threw on a jacket, drove swiftly down to the garden centre and sought out the wise minds he had known for years.

'Hard to say, George, but could be he likes delphiniums to do his business in. Some cats do like certain plants.'

George's nerves were frayed to shreds. He sighed,

'Is there nothing I can do except dig up my lovely delphiniums? Why should I have to fashion my garden for next door's blasted cat?'

'Lion's urine, George, that's the answer.'

'So where do I get lion's urine? The nearest safari park's miles away.'

'No problem; pellets, pure concentrated lion's pee. Put them around your delphiniums. Won't hurt them. If the cat thinks there's a much bigger cat lurking around he'll run like hell, mark my words.'

George placed the pellets carefully, wearing rubber gloves so that the monster would detect no human hand.

At 4 am there was no sign of a white blob. Neither was there any garden damage the next morning. Saladin had certainly come into the garden, his paw prints were to be seen, but one whiff of lion had sent him running for cover.

George was almost delirious with happiness. At last, something was working. Amelia had her old George back.

Despite the Big Cat success, George did not let up his nightly 4 am vigil for almost a week. During this time Saladin was to be seen occasionally frolicking, but on his own lawn. But alas, happiness was shortlived. Only eight days after the pellets were put down, George fancied he saw a white blob on the patio again. It was obvious the potency of the lion's waterworks was diminishing, but Saladin's nerve was not. He was spoiling for another delphinium outrage.

'But he must have gone in his own garden, George, so the chances are he'll go back there,' Amelia noted. 'Don't worry.'

But George did worry… He bought more lion pellets, and tried to think of yet more solutions, although scattering the contents of a lion's bladder over his garden was not the way he had envisaged spending his retirement.

It was at about 3 o'clock on the following Saturday afternoon that Shirley called on Amelia. George was in the garden. About an hour later he was summoned indoors, for tea he hoped.

In the sitting room, heaped into a corner of the settee, was a flushed, tear-stained Shirley. No one spoke for several moments. It was clear something was very wrong.

Amelia started… 'Shirley has some bad news, dear…'

Shirley looked up at George, her eyes welling up ready for another outpouring.

'Shirley, what's the matter? What's happened?'

'He's dead, George. He's dead!' And the poor woman fell into Amelia's arms sobbing piteously.

'Good, God. Colin?'

Amelia, cradling Shirley's trembling head on her ample shoulder looked at George, cautioning him. 'No dear, not Colin. It's Shirley's cat. You remember, Saladin. He was run over by the carpet van.'

A curious expression spread across George's face, before he adjusted it to one of compassion. 'Oh, dear, I'm so sorry Shirley. Yes, I know, you get so fond of them. We've been through all that, haven't we, Amelia? Our old dog, you know. That's why we never replaced him. Couldn't. Not worth it, Shirley, believe me. Not worth the…' he paused.

Amelia held her breath.

'…the heartache.'

Shirley dabbed her eyes. 'You are quite right, George. That's what Colin says too. Never again. There could never be another Saladin.'

George patted his grieving neighbour gently on the shoulder and said with the utmost sincerity, 'No, Shirley, there could never be another Saladin. Colin is very wise. Never again; don't even think of it.'

At the door, Shirley, red-eyed and ready to spill new tears, turned to George and Amelia, smiling forlornly, 'He was such a character.'

'Really?' George replied with exaggerated concern. Amelia sidled up to her husband and linked her arm through his, just in case she needed to break it suddenly.

'Do you know…he loved flowers! Loved them! Couldn't get enough of them! Can you believe it?' Shirley trilled.

Prompted by Amelia's pulse stopping grip, George smiled, paused for a moment, and in a voice oozing conviction said, 'Yes, Shirley, oddly enough I can. I really can…'

Reseeding

Cecilia Morreau

It was what my daughter would describe as a 'one-eighty' day. Which doesn't mean it was the sort of day that you score well at darts, nor have a quick spin around Monte Carlo – although if I could have that day again I would definitely have opted for either of those exciting options. No, what she means is that it was the sort of day where you are trolling along quite nicely, heading in one direction, in my case a sunshiny, bird-singy, God's-in-his-heaven route, when suddenly fate picks you up and spins you one hundred and eighty degrees until you find yourself facing a whole different vista, a rainy, stormy, highway completely devoid of feathered friends and helpful deities.

I was digging in the garden, a commonplace activity for me, having spent the good part of the last year taming a wilderness more commonly found in the Amazon than accompanying a South Wales residence. The bad part of the year was spent selling advertising for the local rag. The afternoon in question was a Friday and, I admit, I was skiving. The joy of telesales at the nether end of the week is akin to wringing blood from the proverbial stone. My corpulent and unpleasant boss had left the office to 'network' in the local hostelry, and I had found myself shutting down my computer, grabbing my bag and heading out into the crisp autumn sunshine. My garden called. I had precisely two and a half hours before the kids came in demanding bread products, refreshing beverages and homework help. Adorned in my usual stunning outfit of holey, green, waxed jacket, fashionably mutilated blue jeans, wellington boots of a dubious cleanliness and large leather gloves that made me look like an extra from Gerry Cottle's circus, I was manfully, no, womanfully, attacking the last pocket of wilderness in the grounds of our country estate. Country estate should be construed here as a figure of speech. A more accurate description would be a small terraced, ex-miner's cottage with a long steep strip of garden, on the outskirts of Cardiff.

I had the task of weed clearing down to a fine art, having by this time, had plenty of practice. When I say weeds, do not imagine a few yellow dandelions glowing innocently in the autumn sun or daisies dancing in a ring around a green sward. When I say weeds I mean WEEDS. Huge head-high brambles, in impenetrable thickets, liberally intermingled with robust stinging nettles ready to pounce on any exposed flesh – like those blokes down the pub who believe that pinching bottoms is a recreational sport. Mixed in with these baddies was the notorious giant hogweed, with tap roots that reach the outskirts of Sydney, and whose sap burns and stings like a nasty accident in a chemistry lesson when the teacher has popped out for a fag. Hidden beneath these horrors is the more innocent looking bindweed, which although not dangerous to human life forms is fairly fatal to newly-planted foliage, its boa constrictor tendencies strangling the life sap out of your beloved biennials. Last, but not least, is the not-so-innocuous ground elder. If you didn't know better you might imagine that this could be both a pretty and a useful ground cover plant in any country garden, pretty, divided deep green leaves, whorls of dainty white flowers that waft gently in the spring breeze. Well it is good at ground cover, just too good, it is the Third Reich of the perennial world, mercilessly eradicating impure races such as just about any of the flowers you might want to grow.

That afternoon I swung into action with the precision and accuracy of a mother of quads at nappy changing time. With my handy hand scythe I mowed down the tall stems of the brambles, nettles and hogweed with the enthusiasm of someone who would hopefully never have to do it again. The resulting tangle was piled high onto the squeaky wheelbarrow, trundled to the mountainous compost heap in the corner and flung on with my trusty fork – as the jolly haymakers of yore made hay while the sun shone. Back at the sight of the massacre I threw my fork into the ground beneath the roots of my opponents and stamped on the top of the tines for good measure. Then with all my might, which was considerable after all the training, I levered them out by the roots and shook the soil from them. Each adversary needed a slightly different technique, the nettles came out in long satisfying tangles – like when you pull a corner of the wallpaper and the whole thing comes off in one glorious sheet. The brambles are tough blighters that need a super-levering technique often involving sitting on the end of the fork and bouncing up and down space hopper style. The hogweed's long tap roots needed careful excavation avoiding injuring any innocent Australian citizens in the vicinity. The bindweed is a challenge, its brittle white roots, reminiscent of the bones of a cat I dug up last year, will reroot if the tiniest smidgen is left behind, hence the thoroughness of a toddler's search for the last chocolate button in the packet is required. Finally the clumpy ground elder needs a good twist evocative of the end of an Agatha Christie mystery novel.

Gardening was not my first love, I acquired it by default. Really it was my husband Paul's thing. Before we moved into our current bijou residence we had an allotment, where he would spend many carefree hours whilst I stayed in our flat, fed babies, changed nappies and mopped up general mess and tears. The concept was that if we moved to a place with a nice big garden he would 'be there' for me and the kiddies. Looking back this was probably my concept rather than his. Our new piece of land, as I have mentioned before, was, to say the least, overgrown. Somehow it fell to me to clear this space in order to reshape it into our own little piece of paradise, where children would canter happily in the great outdoors and Paul and I would sip martinis on a quiet summer's evening.

Now, don't get me wrong, I was happy to perform this daring and dangerous service for the good of our family idyll. I only worked part-time, three days a week, at the newspaper, so it could be construed that I had more free hours than Paul, who, although relatively unburdened by the niceties of the washing machine, the Hoover and his offspring, did work full-time. Very full-time. Aside from which his love was my love, his passions my passions, or so I believed. I acquired a great deal of horticultural knowledge, soaking up information about plants, soil, compost, microclimate and the like from books and television with the zeal of your genuine zealot. I knew what to plant where, why and how. Latin taxonomy trips off my tongue as fluently and as quickly, now, as my daughter can text nonsense (txt 0sns) to her friends. The niceties of garden design, colour coordination and hard landscaping hold no fears for me.

So, back to the one-eighty afternoon. I was mid-flow with the fork and compost heap technique when I heard the back door of our house open with its familiar squeak. Oh joy! I thought the beloved spouse home early for a change. It was either that or a burglar, but then again a burglar is hardly likely to come into the back garden when all the valuables are stored inside the house. I flung the last of the wheelbarrow's contents onto the pile and was just removing my clown gloves in preparation for a passionate reunion when I heard voices. I deduced the spouse was not alone, not being a man prone to talking to himself, especially in a woman's voice.

'I've cleared all this; it used to be totally overgrown,' I heard him say. I could not see him, mostly because the compost heap obscured my view – due to the fact that I was hiding behind it in an uncanny piece of foresight. However, I did feel a strong urge to jump out and mention that in fact it was I who had cleared the aforementioned ground.

'That must have been hard work,' the unknown but definitely feminine voice simpered.

'Yeah, bloody hard work, especially the brambles. Still, it keeps me fit and the results are going to be worth it.'

I assumed at this point that he was probably wearing his coat because to claim to be fit and still sport that beer belly was a tad far-fetched. The voices receded slightly, so

I took the opportunity to peer out from my shelter. They were walking back towards the house, slightly hidden by the *Acer* that I had lovingly planted. The spouse stopped by the tree, obviously to relate how he had taken such care with this precious specimen, digging a large hole, lining it with compost, gently splaying out the roots, supporting the trunk with a sturdy stake and religiously watering the tree all summer long. I stepped out, I couldn't take this any longer, I had to let the truth be known. Paul did not see me, however, because they were standing with their backs towards me. At the precise moment I stepped out, he turned and seemed to be gently brushing something off the girl's face, possibly a leaf from my *Acer*...

Whose House is This?

Judith Barrow

I've given up trying to persuade Mum to stay indoors, so here we both are, huddled in a shed no bigger than a telephone box, our breath, white vapour, mingling in the coldest December day this year.

I've wrapped her up as best I can: coat, blankets, woolly hat and gloves. The gloves are the most important; she will insist on trying to touch the shears and secateurs. I've cleaned, sharpened and oiled them and the shine of the blades fascinates her.

'Just let me hold them,' she says for the tenth time after I've put them safely out of her reach.

'Not today, you'll get oil on your coat.' Her hat has fallen over one eye and she tilts her head upwards and glares crossly at me. I straighten it. 'I think we've done enough in here for today.' Ignoring the loud sigh that balloons her cheeks I add, 'Let's go in for a drink.'

Hands under her armpits, I haul her to her feet. The blankets drop to the floor. I kick them to one side; I'll pick them up later. We shuffle out of the door.

'Mind the step. And watch the ice on the path.'

'I can manage, I'm not a baby.'

'I know.' Even so, I hold one hand under her elbow and my other arm around her shoulders. She seems so tiny.

'How about we have a whiskey and hot water to warm us?' We pick up pace towards the back door. Just before we go in, she stops.

'Whose house is this?'

'It's ours, Mum; we've been here thirty years.'

But she won't go in. Stubbornly she holds on to the frame with stiff arms.

'This isn't our door, our door is blue.'

'No, we had double glazing last summer. This is our new back door.'

She doesn't speak. I wait, my hands on her waist. She turns, her arms dropping to her sides; the many layers she wears means that they are at an angle from her body as though she is gesturing in surprise. She looks around the garden.

'Whose house is this?'

'Ours.'

I wait. It's best to keep quiet when she's in one of these moods.

The birds are making short work of the seeds and bread we scattered earlier. The squirrel stares at us, still as a statue, hanging from the peanut holder.

'I don't like winter,' she says. And then in one of her sudden changes of subject, 'Do you remember your granddad's allotment?'

And, in a flash, I'm there.

It's a memory long forgotten. I don't know why or where I've conjured it up from. Perhaps it's the clouds, bruised with threatening rain or hail, just like that day so long ago, or it's the blackbird scuttling around on the lawn. Anyway, there I am, after all this time. Seven years old, sitting on the outside lavatory, picking the whitewash off the wall and watching the blackbird following my grandfather as he digs in his allotment, which is on the other side of the low wall of our yard. He's turning the soil over one last time before winter sets in. I've left the door open. If it's closed the darkness smothers me and I'm afraid; there would be only a thin line of light at the bottom of the door where the wind whistles through and causes goose-bumps on my legs.

Heavy drops begin to fall to the ground, turning into muddy water on the clay soil. My grandfather pushes the peak of his cap off his forehead, squints up at the sky, and takes a tab end of cigarette from behind his ear. He rolls the flattened tip between forefinger and thumb but his hands are wet and the paper quickly becomes saturated. The strands of tobacco fall out. He swears softly, unaware I am there, and takes a small yellow tin from his trouser pocket. Balancing his spade against his leg, he carefully taps the remains of the cigarette into the box.

I lean forward and tear a square of newspaper off the loop of string hanging from the back of the door, use it, and stand to pull up my knickers. The rain slants down in a sudden rush, hitting the flags in the yard with loud slaps. Granddad has disappeared into his shed. I shiver, thread the belt of my navy gabardine coat through the buckle and tighten it. Lowering the wooden lid of the lavatory, I sit on it, waiting for the rain to stop so that I can make a run for the house.

After a few minutes it turns into a drizzle and, as I hesitate, my grandfather reappears to stand in the doorway of the shed. He glances to his left and I follow his gaze. I can hear the muffled clucking of the hens in their shelter in the run at the far side of his allotment. Granddad drags on the gold chain across his chest until he is holding his fob watch in his hands. His lips move with a low breathy whistle… *It's a Long Way to Tipperary.*

If I go now he will see me and know I have been watching him. He hates being watched. A small dour man in poor health, we have lived with him since Grandma died, three years ago. Resentful of his need for my mother, he speaks as little as possible and spends much of his time in his allotment.

He slips the watch back into the pocket in his padded brown waistcoat and begins the laborious process of rolling another cigarette. This always fascinates me and I watch until he finally crouches down to strike a match along the brick that he keeps by the shed door just for that purpose. Cupping his hands he shelters the flame and sucks vigorously. The paper flares for a second and then the tobacco glows red. Slouching against the doorframe, Granddad lifts his chin and, making faces like a fish gulping, blows smoke rings upwards. We both watch as each circle floats away, expanding outwards until it is only a whisp of white against the glowering sky.

Finally he pushes himself upright and strides towards the hen house, flicking the stump of cigarette into the air. It scatters sparks as it arcs away. I stop swinging my legs, uncross my ankles and peep around the door frame. The gate of the hen run is made from chicken wire, stretched over thin pieces of wood. He lifts it on its hinges and squeezes through. He stands still for a minute. The hens become quiet. He bends down, disappearing below the yard wall. There is a sudden commotion and when he stands up he is holding a hen by its legs. I turn my head sideways to look at it. It's Ethel; I recognize her by the black patch of feathers on her wing that contrasts with the auburn ones. She is squawking and flapping frantically.

Somehow I know what is going to happen. I open my mouth to shout but no sound comes out. I begin to run towards Grandad. With a quick twist he snaps her neck before I reach the gate.

'Yes,' I say to Mum. 'Yes, I remember Granddad's allotment.'

Mum and I are vegetarians. I have been for as long as I can remember; Mum, since I started doing the cooking ten years ago.

Today we are planning to plant shallot and onion sets into the vegetable patch and to transfer the small tomato plants I've grown from seed, into Gro-Bags, in the greenhouse.

It's cool for the beginning of May. The pale sun struggles through a skein of lemon clouds and a chilly breeze causes the line of *Leylandii* in next door's garden to shiver constantly but in the shelter of our fence it's pleasant and, in the greenhouse, quite warm. Mum is sitting, muffled up as usual, in her chair, just outside the doorway.

'Warm enough?'

She doesn't answer and, when I kneel down at her side, I see she is asleep; gentle snores bubbling her lips. I tuck her hands under the blanket and take the opportunity to carry the Gro-Bags from the shed to the greenhouse. The rattle of the wheelbarrow doesn't wake her and I manage to get most of the tomato plants transferred before she starts to move restlessly, muttering to herself. Standing up I wipe my hands on my trousers and then kneel next to her, waiting for her to open her eyes. She gets frightened if she can't see me at once.

'Tea?'

'Whose house is this?'

'Tea?' I ask again and she nods, touching my cheek.

We sit on the bench outside the back door, holding hands, waiting for the kettle to boil.

'I'll have to have a wash before I make the tea.' But she won't let go of my fingers. I hear the kettle switch off. 'Just let me make the tea. I'm only in the kitchen.'

But as soon as I disappear she cries out.

'Joyce…Joyce? Whose house is this? Joyce?'

'Won't be a minute. Watch the birds. And just look at the *Clematis*; that plant, next to you in the tub. It's never had so many flowers on it. Isn't it pretty?' I keep talking but she still calls my name. Hurriedly I brew, put two cups, a jug of milk, a packet of digestives and the teapot on the tray. The phone rings, 'No, thanks, I don't need double glazing, nor a conservatory,' but the woman is persistent and keeps talking, so in the end I put the receiver down on her. 'Coming now, Mum.' There is no answer. I look out of the window but can't see her.

'Mum?'

She's not there. I hurry to the greenhouse, then the shed. A quick look around the garden proves fruitless. She's nowhere to be seen. The gate's swinging open.

I run down the lane. There isn't a footpath and I hope there are no boy racers trying the twists and turn, of our narrow road today. The scent of the bluebells mixes with that of the wild garlic; the vivid blue diminished by the prolific cowslip.

And there she is. I can hardly believe it; she is walking

quite quickly in her pink fluffy slippers. Her white hair flows down her back and from the way she's waving her arms around I can tell she's upset, even before I hear her crying. There's a wet patch on the back of her skirt so that the material clings to her skinny buttocks.

'Mum.'

She doesn't hear me.

My breath is shallow; I'm not as young as I was. I catch up with her, careful not to touch or frighten her.

'Mum?'

She stops and looks at me, sobbing; tears and snot mingle.

'Lost,' she says, 'lost.'

'No, you're not lost. I'm here now. Come on, let's go home.' She won't move. She prods me in the chest.

'No,' she says, 'no. Joyce, Joyce…lost…again. Always getting lost.'

'No, I'm here, Mum. See, I'm here. It's me, Joyce.' She hesitates, shaking her head. I say again, 'Your daughter, Joyce. I'm here.'

She pushes me away, flapping her hands at me.

'Not Joyce. Joyce…little. My little girl…lost. Frightened…without me…ends in tears.'

And I know what she means. When I was young, I would slip away from her in town; eager to explore but, inevitably, I would finish up being frightened by the freedom I had gained. Scared and alone and surrounded by strangers.

'Oh, that Joyce,' I say, 'that Joyce. She's back at the house, she came back.'

She stares at me suspiciously. 'Came back? Never gets back…can't get back.' Looking into her eyes, the blue faded by years, I see a flicker of comprehension as she repeats, '…can never get back.'

I hold out my hand to her. Through the thin material of her cotton gloves, her fingers feel cold. And even though I know I am lying, I say firmly. 'It's never too late to go back, Mum. Now, let's go home for that cup of tea.'

On the drive the cherry blossom floats its flowers down on us.

'It's a wedding,' she laughs.

And catches a petal.

The rain pounds heavily on the porch roof and when I open the door it gusts in with me. Mum, sitting in the wheelchair lent to us by Social Services, shouts, 'Shut.' She shouts a lot these days. She hates being inside but weeks of dull, grey days and rain have stopped us from going outside and, for some inexplicable reason, being in the greenhouse now frightens her, so things in there have been neglected. The garden has suffered, too. The grass on the lawn is inches long. It never dries out enough to be mown. The flower beds are a flattened slimy mess and the riot of colour that was spring has degenerated under one of the worst summers I can remember.

Sometimes I feel that there is a scream waiting to burst from my mouth; one, which if I let it escape, will never stop.

'What a day,' I say, not expecting an answer. I straighten the blanket over her knees but she throws it off and punches my arm. Yet another bruise to add to the others.

'Whose house…this?'

She's wearing the purple satin evening gloves she once

wore to a mayor's ball she went to with Dad. She found them a few days ago, in a charity bag I'd put in the hall for the church jumble sale.

'Mine,' she'd shouted, triumphantly. She refuses to take them off.

'Biscuit,' she yells now, 'tea and biscuit.'

'In a minute, Mum.' I speak sharper than I meant to but I'm tired. Last night's full moon had lit up the fuchsia outside her bedroom and the strong breeze that's been blowing all week had whipped the branches around. The shadows had frightened her and kept her awake. I'm going to cut the bloody thing down.

'It's that fuck you thingy,' she'd cried, 'it's getting in.'

'Fuchsia, Mum,' I'm sure she knows what she's saying. Long ago, a family friend, a Polish woman, had visited and admired the shrubs in the garden, 'especially the fuckyas' she'd enunciated carefully. Dad had left the room but we heard his guffaws as he went down the hall and it had become a family joke.

'Fuck you,' Mum says obstinately.

Like I say, sometimes I swear she knows what she's saying.

I bring in the last of the tomatoes. It's been a poor year. They are tiny and green. I could throw them away but old habits die hard.

'I'll make chutney out of these.'

She doesn't answer; she's lost in her own world.

I was never a cook. Mum had insisted on trying to teach me, years ago but had failed.

'You'll need to attract a man somehow,' she'd said, 'with

your looks you'll have to find something that will make them want to stay.' Lately, the more I think about it, the more I realise how spiteful she was when I was younger. I should have left her years ago.

It's too late now. I look through the kitchen window; there are some panes missing in the greenhouse. They were blown out in a gale, a few weeks ago and I haven't bothered doing anything about it. I'm waiting for another storm; hopefully one that will flatten the bloody thing.

I put Mum in the lounge, in front of the television.

'Not our house,' she mumbles.

I ignore her.

Alan Titchmarsh is telling her it's time to tidy the garden before the long winter months. He's always so damn cheerful.

I'm not going to bother with the garden next year, it's more trouble than it's worth. I brew the tea and pour Mum's into the beaker with the spout. I make myself a sandwich, take a bite and throw it in the bin. I'm not hungry. I mash a banana for her. I don't rush; she's no sense of day or night anymore and wants to eat all the time. She's put on a lot of weight. I've lost two stones and I am so tired. I haven't been sleeping much and when I do I have nightmares. I wish Mum hadn't reminded me about Granddad and Ethel. She'd laughed, all those years ago, when I told her what he'd done. Said not to be so soft.

It's starting to rain again.

Last night I killed my mother.

I could say I didn't want her to go into a home.

Or the thought of winter depresses me.

But, to be truthful, I'd had enough. I couldn't carry on.

It would have been easier to smother her. But it seemed right, somehow.

It was so easy; just one quick twist.

She never liked winter anyway.

Biographical Notes

Sue Anderson is a teacher. She always meant to write, but only started when she came to Wales twenty-odd years ago. Since then she has written short stories, poems and articles, some of which are published, and has even attempted the odd novel. Now that she is semi-retired there is supposed to be more time for writing, but it doesn't seem to work out that way.

Sue has a story in the Honno's *Mirror Mirror* anthology and is very pleased to be a Honno author again.

Naomi Bagel was born in Shoreham-by-Sea, Sussex. A dyslexic, she left school early having taken no exams.

Naomi worked as an archaeologist in Southampton. She has been self-employed for many years, running her own second-hand and recycling shop. Naomi has a wide and varied work experience which includes farm work, catering, and presenting workshops to groups, and she has been involved in many aspects of outdoor events from Glastonbury festival to Green Gatherings and many other music and arts events.

Naomi enjoys reading, walking, history, and has always written stories and poems. She is currently finishing an MA course in creative writing.

She has been published in the anthology *A Haunting Touch* (Parthian), also in Cambrensis and Roundy House, and she has distributed two books of self-published poetry.

Judith Barrow grew up in a small village in the Pennines and moved to Pembrokeshire in 1978. She has a BA in

Literature and an MA in Creative Writing. Her work has appeared in previous Honno anthologies. She has had short stories, reviews and articles published throughout the British Isles. She has won poetry competitions including the 2004 Roundyhouse Annual Competition and the Lansker Prize for humorous poetry. She has written several plays; one of which was performed in the 'Play Off' competition at the Dylan Thomas Centre in Swansea and has a short screenplay currently in the process of being filmed. She has completed two books for children and at the moment is writing the final draft of her third children's novel. Judith was shortlisted in the Cinnamon Press Award for her second adult novel: a saga set in the Second World War.

Hilary Bowers is divorced and lives alone in a pretty village situated a short distance from Aberystwyth. Although Yorkshire born and bred she has lived in Wales for nineteen years. She works full-time as the manager of the Salvation Army 'Care and Share' charity shop in Aberystwyth. Her main hobby is acting with the 'Castaways' community theatre based at Aberystwyth Arts Centre, and she also attends Chinese Dance classes, but her real love is writing, which she has been doing continuously for over six years; initially using creative writing classes as a springboard but for the past few years jointly co-ordinating a weekly informal writers' and artists' self-help group.

Hilary divides her writing time between long-term novel projects and daily additions to her latest short stories.

Alexandra Claire was born and brought up in Cardiff. She trained at London Contemporary Dance School before working as a dancer and choreographer throughout Europe. Alexandra has had short stories published in anthologies and in the press. Alexandra received the Dance Critique Award in 2007. She is currently writing her first novel with the support of an Academi Writer's Bursary.

Sue Coffey is from Aberdare. Following sundry wanderings, over the hills and far away, with her family, she has recently moved to a village outside Cardiff. She works for a training association and moonlights as a creative writing tutor for Cardiff University.

Since she began writing 'properly' in 2001 her stories have won competitions or been shortlisted, most recently for the Legend Writing Award 2007. She has been published in anthologies and national magazines. Sue is often to be found fondly imagining the day she publishes a collection of short stories; sees the novel in print; hears the radio play; breaks up fistfights between rival publishers competing for her signature on the dotted line…

Siân Melangell Dafydd was bought up at the foot of the Berwyn and has the waters of the Dyfrdwy running in her veins.

Her work includes poetry, prose and essays for *Planet*, *New Welsh Review*, *Taliesin* and *Tu Chwith*. She has contributed to *Laughing not Laughing* (Honno), *Storïau'r Troad* (Gomer) and *Hon: Ynys y Galon* (Gomer).

Ella-Louise Gilbert. Born in 1983, she grew up in the picturesque village of Mumbles, where there were colourful carnivals and eccentric characters to inspire any writer. She graduated with a Masters in Creative and Media Writing at Swansea University, taught by Welsh writers Stevie Davies and Nigel Jenkins. She is a regular reviewer for the Theatre Wales website where one's efforts are repaid in free wine! She is a member of Swansea Little Theatre and is thoroughly enjoying playing the title role in their current panto, *Sleeping Beauty*. This short story is her first publication. When she grows up, she wants to be tall.

Imogen Rhia Herrad was born and brought up in Germany and writes in German and English. She has lived in Wales (where she learnt Welsh), London and Argentina, and currently divides her time between Cardiff and Berlin.

Her programmes for German public radio include pieces about the Queen of Sheba, Morgan le Fay, Zora Neale Hurston, the Mapuche people of Patagonia, and the cultural histories of sheep, dragons, the apple and the figure of the hermaphrodite, respectively. Her collection of short stories inspired by the legends of Welsh women saints, *The Woman who loved an Octopus and other Saints' Tales* was published in 2007 by Seren Books.

Imogen's current projects include a crime novel set in London and Wales, and a narrative of her travels in *Y Wladfa*, the Welsh settlements in Patagonia.

Christine Hirst. Sadly, this is Christine's last story for Honno. She died on October 6th 2007 before seeing 'Jonesy's Place' in print. Writing was very important to her and she coped bravely with severe illness over many years. She fought to complete the things that mattered to her and her spirit remained buoyant throughout.

Ruth Joseph is from Cardiff. She graduated with an MPhil in Writing from Glamorgan University, and was approached by Accent Press to publish *Red Stilettos*, her collection of short stories. She is a Rhys Davies and Cadenza prizewinner, and won the Lichfield Short Story Prize. She has had work published by Honno, Accent Press, *New Welsh Review*, *Loki*, and *Cambrensis*. Her memoir, *Remembering Judith*, chronicles her situation as child carer to an anorexic mother traumatised from the after-effects of the Holocaust. Her husband Mervyn, family and rescue Labrador are a source of inspiration, and comfort.

Vivien Kelly. After the publication of her first novel, Vivien Kelly left a career as a counsellor in London to live on Achill, a remote island off the coast of County Mayo. On finding that this setting was only conducive to writing erotica, she moved to Pembrokeshire.

She was one of the first cohort of students to complete the Creative and Media Writing MA at Swansea University, from which she graduated with distinction and a new appreciation of poetry.

She is presently living in Brynamman, working on her next novel, and fashioning a living as tutor, therapist, performer, writing coach and life coach.

Elizabeth Morgan was born in Llanelli, became a teacher and immediately trained for the theatre. There followed stage, television and the BBC Drama Repertory Company – when she began to write. She has written some 26 plays for Radio Four, a few for television and toured the UK and the USA with her two one-woman plays. Elizabeth has appeared in dozens of shows and serials including 'Dad's Army'; was in 'The Old Devils' for BBC Wales and recorded 'Under Milk Wood' with Anthony Hopkins. In May 2007 her fourth book *Life Style French Style* (How To Books) was published. She lives in France most of the year, and contributes monthly articles to 'French News', for whom she anticipates covering the Wales/France international in March. Currently working on a novel about Patagonia.

A Ddraig Goch flies from the balcony of her French home; anyone welcome…

Cecilia Morreau is a director of Leaf Books, a small independent publishing company based in South Wales – www.leafbooks.co.uk. She has a degree in Creative Writing from Glamorgan University and is currently finishing her MPhil. She is also writing a sitcom, another novel, and a shopping list. Her poetry collection is well-known for not having been published and her blog (www.ceciliamorreau.blogspot.com) is notorious for reasons best not understood. She has a garden, some children, a shed and a great deal of dust lurking in unreachable places. Previous existences saw her running a restaurant, being a yoga teacher, performing in a circus, catching ping-pong balls on her nose and other stuff that she can't remember. Her latest exciting project is Mostly Life, a comedy website that aims to encapsulate all things mirthful in one handily delicious package – www.mostlylife.com. Coming soon to a screen near you…

Catherine Osborn is a retired schoolteacher and actress living near Regent's Park in London. She was brought up in the Rhondda Valley and remained there until going to college in her twenties. She returns at least twice a year to visit relatives and friends.

She has always enjoyed writing, and retirement gives her the opportunity. She has written children's novels as well as several short stories, some of which have been published or won prizes in competition. She is putting together a collection of stories that she hopes to get published.

Molly Price was born in Pembroke in 1931. She was educated at Pembroke Dock Grammar School and after passing her Civil Service exams she lived and worked in Manchester, where she met her husband, Alwyn. She returned to Pembrokeshire in 1967 to bring up her three children and worked in local libraries for many years. Molly was always an avid reader and became a prolific writer in her retirement. She was a keen member of the Pembroke Dock Creative Writing Group and in 2005 obtained a Certificate of Higher Education in Creative Writing from Trinity College, Carmarthen. Her love of gardening and nature was often reflected in her stories and poetry. She was also known for her naughty sense of humour and 'Coming Up Roses', her first published work, beautfully showcases both of these important elements in her life.

Sadly Molly died in September 2007. However we are very pleased to have helped her achieve one of her ambitions – to be a published writer.

Nina Schmieder is co-author of a non-fiction book and has worked as a magazine editor and a TV producer;

experiences that have helped shape her writing, which often contains the recurring theme of hybrid lifestyles and the alienation of immigrant women from native as well as host cultures. Although the past haunts the present, the two often run on parallel tracks, rarely merging or unifying, resulting in life long pain of non-belonging and displacement.

A first generation immigrant herself, Nina is interested in the 'narrativisation' of the South Asian immigrant women's experiences in the postcolonial English language literature. She has lived in the UK, United States and in Canada. She is currently working on a novel and her memoirs.

Ally Thomas was born in Skewen. Married to Ken, she has two sons and a granddaughter. Graduating as a mature student from Swansea University's DACE in 2005, she won the Anna Marie Taylor Prize for outstanding contribution to the arts. She is a 'Martini' writer – writing anytime, anyplace and about anything. Keenly interested in politics, she is currently a local councillor. She co-wrote and sang lead as a mermaid in a musical performed in Taliesin, Swansea, about a Wales Tourist Board scam. She is Chair of Peacock Vein Script Shop and regularly contributes to *Seventh Quarry Poetry* magazine.

Joy Tucker is a Scottish writer who has lived in Wales for many years. Her first story was published in the 1960s and she has been writing ever since. A former columnist and feature writer with the *Glasgow Herald*, her short stories have been published in anthologies, newspapers and magazines throughout Britain. Some have been broadcast on BBC Radio 4. Joy's radio credits include children's stories and poems, some of which she wrote for her own son and daughter. Now she writes them for her grandchildren. Recently, Joy has turned to playwriting, with plays produced at the Landmark Theatre, Ilfracombe, the Dylan Thomas Centre in Swansea and performances by amateur groups in Chichester and Gower. Her one-act drama 'Top Table' was awarded 'Best Play' in the first Swansea Bay Film Festival in 2006.

Joy lives on the Gower Peninsula with her Welsh husband.

PennyAnne Windsor lived in Wales for many years teaching creative writing and literature. In 2003 she returned to Somerset to work – creating stories and poetry with groups of disabled people – as Writer-in-Residence with Take Art! who published her most recent collection of poems *On the Edges of My Skirt* in 2004.

Widely published as a poet and short story writer she continues to work as a story teller, co-writing a book about medieval Somerset churches, and a collection of her own Cypriot and Greek poems *Shaking the Almond Tree*. She lives in the Mendip Hills with her husband.

Other Short Story Anthologies
from Honno

Safe World Gone

Edited by Patricia Duncker and Janet Thomas

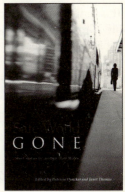

What would it take to change your world? In this exciting diverse anthology with stories that are by turns funny, touching and scary, Welsh women authors explore the turning points that can change a woman's life forever.

ISBN 978-1-870206-77-8

Mirror Mirror

Edited by Patricia Duncker and Janet Thomas

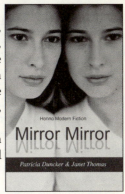

The wars between women – wife and mistress, first and second wife, mother and daughter, Welsh and English, the stay-at-home and the working mother – are fought out with fresh energy in this collection. Equally vivid is the longing – for lovers, fantasies, mothers, dreams, and for the other women we wish we were.

Includes stories from Patricia Duncker, Elin ap Hywel, Jo Mazelis, Ann Oosthuizen and Jenny Sullivan.

ISBN 978-1-870206-57-0

My Cheating Heart

Edited by Kitty Sewell

There's nothing foreign to the human heart, but there's lots that's forbidden and plenty that's hidden...

This anthology, collected on the theme of infidelity, includes work by Jo Verity, Jenny Sullivan, Ruth Joseph, and Melanie Mauthner, and each of the writers has fashioned a gem from the grit in the oyster of the human heart.

ISBN 978-1-879296-73-0

Autobiographical Anthologies from Honno

Strange Days Indeed

Edited by Lindsay Ashford & Rebecca Tope

Motherhood is a strange country – you can't tell what it's going to be like until you get there and you have no idea how long the journey is going to be. Funny, shocking and tender, this is a unique collection of autobiographical writings about motherhood, covering the whole spectrum of what it means to be a mother - from getting pregnant to the empty-nest syndrome.

ISBN 978-1-870206-83-9

Even the Rain is Different

Edited by Gwyneth Tyson Roberts

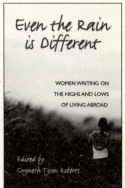

From sleeping in trees in Corsica to escaping Stalinist purges in Moscow. From Southern Europe to South America, Russia to Australia. Welsh Women write on the highs and lows of living abroad. These fascinating accounts of lives spent abroad in the past 150 years are a true celebration of the mix of cultural experience that makes the modern Welsh woman.

ISBN 978-1-870206-63-1

ABOUT HONNO

Honno Welsh Women's Press was set up in 1986 by a group of women who felt strongly that women in Wales needed wider opportunities to see their writing in print and to become involved in the publishing process. Our aim is to develop the writing talents of women in Wales, give them new and exciting opportunities to see their work published and often to give them their first 'break' as a writer.

Honno is registered as a community co-operative. Any profit that Honno makes is invested in the publishing programme. Women from Wales and around the world have expressed their support for Honno by buying shares in the co-operative. Shareholders' liability is limited to the amount invested and each shareholder has a vote at the Annual General Meeting.

To buy shares or to receive further information about forthcoming publications, please write to Honno at the address below, or visit our website: **www.honno.co.uk**.

Honno
'Ailsa Craig'
Heol y Cawl
Dinas Powys
Bro Morgannwg
CF64 4AH